Praise for Marie Miranda Cruz's *Everlasting Nora*

A Junior Library Guild Selection
A *Kirkus Reviews* Best Books of 2018 Selection
Silver Medal in the Parents' Choice Awards
Bank Street's Best Children's Books of the Year for 12–14

"A story of friendship and unrelenting hope. Readers will escape into a world unlike any other, and will be better for it."
— Erin Entrada Kelly,
Newbery Award–winning author

"Heartwarming and fun, with a fresh twist and a diverse cast of characters!"
—Melissa de la Cruz,
#1 *New York Times* bestselling author

"Woah! Marie Cruz's vivid writing transported me into a thrilling, memorable adventure!"
—Alex Gino

"Cruz offers an important and engaging tale. . . . At its heart, this is a story about friendship and family—the one we're born into and the one we make. . . . This moving title should find a place in all libraries looking for authentic and powerful middle-grade stories."
—*School Library Journal* (starred review)

"Nora's story is a tribute to Filipino children, and readers of all backgrounds will find themselves immersed in the culture, learning bits of Tagalog and longing to savor the delicacies described throughout such as biko, champorado, and banana-que. Cruz's touching debut breathes life, beauty, and everlasting hope into a place where danger lurks and the dead rest."

—*Kirkus Reviews* (starred review)

"This impactful debut novel shows young readers the devastating reality of life for some children in the world, introduces them to a new language and culture, and demonstrates the power of family and neighbors, courage, hope, and, most of all, perseverance."

—*Booklist*

"Cruz's rich descriptions of Filipino culture intensify the sense of place and proffer bright spots in Nora's difficult situation."

—*Publishers Weekly*

"Debut author Cruz is a writer and scientist who uses her own Filipino background to infuse this book with authentic texture. . . . Living in Manila's main cemetery is difficult for Nora but, because of her personal strength and aided by good friends, she perseveres in this debut middle-grade novel."

—*Shelf Awareness*

Everlasting Nora

MARIE MIRANDA CRUZ

A TOM DOHERTY ASSOCIATES BOOK

NEW YORK

This is a work of fiction. All of the characters, organizations, and events portrayed in this novel are either products of the author's imagination or are used fictitiously.

EVERLASTING NORA

Copyright © 2018 by Marie Miranda Cruz

Reader's guide copyright © 2018 by Tor Books

All rights reserved.

A Starscape Book
Published by Tom Doherty Associates
120 Broadway
New York, NY 10271

www.tor-forge.com

The Library of Congress has cataloged the hardcover edition as follows:

Names: Cruz, Marie Miranda, author.
Title: Everlasting Nora / Marie Miranda Cruz.
Description: First edition. | New York : [Starscape]/Tom Doherty Associates, 2018.
Identifiers: LCCN 2018044342| ISBN 9780765394590 (hardcover : alk. paper) | ISBN 9781250314680 (international, sold outside the U.S., subject to rights availability) | ISBN 9780765394613 (ebook)
Subjects: | CYAC: Missing persons—Fiction. | Homeless persons—Fiction. | Poverty—Fiction. | Cemeteries—Fiction. | Manila (Philippines)—Fiction. | Philippines—Fiction.
Classification: LCC PZ7.1.C795 Eve 2018 | DDC [Fic]—dc23
LC record available at https://lccn.loc.gov/2018044342

ISBN 978-0-7653-9460-6 (trade paperback)

Our books may be purchased in bulk for promotional, educational, or business use. Please contact your local bookseller or the Macmillan Corporate and Premium Sales Department at 1-800-221-7945, extension 5442, or by email at MacmillanSpecialMarkets@macmillan.com.

First Edition: October 2018
First Trade Paperback Edition: March 2020

Printed in the United States of America

0 9 8 7 6 5 4 3 2 1

To Nellie and Ed, the best parents a girl can have

Acknowledgments

This book is very special to me because it is the first novel I ever wrote. It began as a tiny wish in my heart and has become the fulfillment of my dreams.

Many thanks a thousand times over to my lovely agent, Paula Munier, who never stopped believing in me as a writer, who loved and supported my work, and who never tired in her pursuit to find a home for my books.

I am ever grateful to my editor, Diana M. Pho, for sharing her wisdom. Her excellent vision guided me as I worked to shape this book you have in your hands today. Thank you so much for making my first foray into publishing an experience I will never forget and one I've learned so much from.

To Zohra Ashpari, thank you for your insightful feedback, for your unrelenting support, and for welcoming me to New York City with cookies. They were delicious!

To the entire Tor team, thank you for the many months of care and hard work you've put into making this author's dream come true.

To my sensitivity readers, Day Cabuhat, Ruby Kalaw,

and Joanna Fabicon, you have my heartfelt gratitude and appreciation for your time and discerning comments.

To my critique partners past and present, Stephanie Denise Brown, Carlynn Whitt, Edith Cohn, Erin Fry, Rosa Leyva, Emily Allen, and Nicole Popel, thank you for your years of friendship, commiserating cups of coffee, and astute feedback. I couldn't have asked for better writers to take this journey with.

To my friends at SCBWI, many thanks for the camaraderie and supportive community. You know who you are.

To Nova Ren Suma and my Djerassi sisters—you are all amazing women and authors! You have become such wonderful friends. I feel so honored and blessed to be in your company. Thank you for all the conversations and glasses of wine over the years.

Many thanks to Rosemary King for taking the time to answer my questions about garment industry labor practices in the Philippines.

To my mother, Nellie Miranda; my mother-in-law, Ely Cruz; Marissa Jew; and May Oropesa, thank you for all the memories you've shared and for being on hand when I needed clarification about all things Filipino.

To my children, Gabe and Abi, thank you for being the perfect sounding boards for my seemingly endless parade of story ideas and plot questions. It is you whose opinion I valued most in all things, you who encouraged me when I wanted to give up, you who helped make dinner when I was on deadline. You are the loves of my life!!

Finally, to my husband, my Jedi Knight, my rock, Obi Cruz, who puts up with my many books, my baskets of yarn, and my notebook collection, who takes me to historic libraries, who patiently waits while I browse through a bookstore for hours, who fills in for me at home when I need time to write, who carries me through tough times and celebrates with me through good ones—thank you, my love!

Chapter One

IF SOMEONE WERE TO ASK ME TO DESCRIBE A HOME,
I would tell them this.

A home never floods during a typhoon.

A home has a kitchen with a stove for cooking rice.

A home does not have dead people inside it.

These thoughts bounced around in my head while I
walked home through the North Cemetery. It was the
largest one in the city of Manila, maybe in the entire archi-
pelago of the Philippine Islands.

I'd spent the day selling garlands of dried flowers—
everlasting daisies—on a street corner in front of the
cemetery gates. On the way home, I'd stopped at a food stand
to buy dinner: steamed rice and dried salted fish. While I

was there, a pebble had lodged itself in a hole at the bottom of my rubber slippers, and it now poked my heel with every step. But I didn't stop to take it out. I kept moving to keep myself from staring too long at the cemetery visitors and comparing my T-shirt and faded pink shorts with their nice clothes, my dirty slippers with their shiny shoes, and the darkness of my skin with their pale complexions.

Squatter. The unspoken word stabbed me as keenly as the pebble under my foot.

I walked deeper into the sementeryo. The grave houses in this part of the cemetery were smaller and shabbier. There were small children playing hide-and-seek between the tombs. Some kids were standing on top of them, tossing a ball made of old newspapers wrapped in twine. There were men and women, either sweeping out mausoleums or fetching buckets of water for drinking or washing. Others carried whatever food they could buy that day. These people weren't visitors. They *lived* here.

Like me.

Up ahead, I saw Efren Pena and his pushcart classroom on the corner. He waved a book in the air when he saw me. A wide smile dimpled his cheek. He called out, "Nora, join us! We're doing math today."

I waved back at him. A surge of excitement filled me. Last week, we'd learned about Andres Bonifacio and the Philippine Revolution of 1896. Working on math would be fun. Papa had always said I was good with numbers.

Kuya Efren had recently cut his hair. What used to be

thick, black, and wavy was now so short it stuck out all over his head. The cart had a blackboard on one side with math problems written in chalk. On the other, it said *Outreach Education on Wheels* in bright blue letters. I called him Kuya, which means "older brother." It was a way to show him respect.

A few boys and girls were already sitting on plastic mats Kuya had brought, studying the math problems on the blackboard. Kuya Efren beckoned me over. He came to the cemetery a few times a week to teach children whose parents couldn't even afford to send them to public school. They were squatter kids like me who had no money for uniforms and school supplies.

Yes, it would be nice to sit a while and pretend I was back in school. And I could finally pick that small rock out from the bottom of my slipper.

A few more kids arrived. Kuya Efren handed out a workbook, each of us receiving a different color, depending on how much we already knew. I loved solving word problems because they had been my father's favorite. I did three of them. My favorite one was:

Pedro bought 8 ball caps, one for each of his eight friends, for 8 pesos each. The cashier charged him an additional 12 pesos and 7 centavos in sales tax. He left the store with 5 pesos and 93 centavos. How much money did Pedro start with?

The answer was so easy.

Papa used to help me with my homework every night. Remembering him made me wish I hadn't been so lazy when I used to go to a real school. Back then, I hadn't enjoyed math. It was a class I had to get through until it was time to work in our school garden. I closed my eyes. It had been a year since I left school. More than a year since the fire.

I finished the section of math problems and handed the book to Kuya Efren to check. Sitting on the mat next to me was a little boy named Ernie, who lived in a grave house close to mine. I hadn't noticed him at first, because he'd had his back to me. Now he turned and nudged me with his elbow; his dark eyes looked large in his thin face.

"Hey, Nora, how did you finish so fast? I've been sitting here for hours!" He scratched his head with his pencil, pointing to a page in his workbook. "I hate adding and subtracting."

I peered over his shoulder. Ernie had worked through most of the addition problems. I nudged him back and said, "You're almost done! And stop complaining. You have to learn so you can count money. Do you want people to cheat you?"

"I guess not. Real school must be terrible. I'm glad my mother doesn't make me do this every day." He sighed, then bent over his page.

"Real school can be fun too. At my old school, we studied math, grammar, and history, and we also learned how to plant vegetables and fruit."

"Growing plants sounds boring." He scowled, using his fingers to count.

"Well, we also made baskets and played games outside." I nudged him again with my elbow.

He looked at me, his face scrunched up. "Ow! Your elbows are sharp!"

"Oh, stop being a baby!" I leaned in and whispered, "Sometimes, our teacher would give us something special if we got all our spelling words correct. If you do your problems right, Kuya Efren might give you a prize."

Ernie's eyes widened. He mouthed, *Really?*

I nodded. This was only the third time he'd sat down to do schoolwork with the pushcart classroom. He used to watch from a distance, perched on top of a tomb, biting his nails. He had been sitting too far away to see Kuya hand his students a piece of candy every time they completed a math or reading exercise.

"So did you have a lot of friends at school?" Ernie asked, putting down his pencil to use all his fingers to count this time.

"Not a lot. I did have a best friend named Evelyn. We both loved fried bananas so much that we would sneak out of our school during recess so we could buy banana-que. The street vendor was an old woman with no teeth." I still remembered her baskets of fried saba bananas crusted with melted brown sugar on barbecue sticks, and salty fried peanuts with garlic.

Ernie licked his lips as if he could taste it. "Hmm, my favorite!"

"We would buy our snack and eat it fast so we wouldn't

get caught. Sometimes, we would sneak back to school with crumbs of fried brown sugar on our uniform ties and get into trouble anyway."

The memory always made me smile. I wondered if Evelyn would recognize me if she saw me now. My hair was longer. My skin had darkened from standing in the sun selling everlasting-daisy garlands. I didn't think she would. And that was fine. I missed her, but I didn't want her to see me or ask me where I lived or where I went to school.

Kuya Efren tapped me on the shoulder. "Good work, Nora. Would you like to continue with the next page?"

"Salamat, Kuya, but I should go. I have to go home and make more garlands." I picked up the bag that held my dinner. I hadn't eaten since breakfast and thinking about food made my mouth water. "I'll be back next week."

I stood to go and was about to say goodbye when Kuya handed me a battered book of Filipino folktales and a piece of candy wrapped in bright orange paper. I was tempted to eat it then and there, but I resisted. I wanted to save it for something special.

"We are going to practice reading comprehension next week. Read this so you can answer questions about the stories when you come back." Kuya smiled and then turned to help Ernie with his math.

I clutched the book to my chest. It felt good to hold one again. I missed going to a real school. I missed the smell of chalk. Most of all, I missed my best friend. If I saved enough money I could buy a couple of secondhand uniforms, some notebooks, and pencils. I would go back to school next year. I'd have to repeat sixth grade, but that was okay.

Soon. I patted the bump in my pocket. I ran the rest of the way home, wondering if Mama was already there, if she'd brought home anything good to eat. It was a Sunday, after all, which meant it was time for our once-a-week treat of something sweet, like a nice, ripe mango or a slice of biko, a kind of sticky rice cake topped with caramelized coconut cream frosting wrapped in a banana leaf.

But she wasn't home yet. My grave house was empty. It wasn't a real house, of course, but a mausoleum. It had three walls and a roof made of concrete like a house. The fourth wall was made of iron bars and covered the front of the grave house where the middle opened like a gate. The roof had a square hole covered with glass to let in natural light. I sighed. Papa had loved sunny places. Golden sunlight flickered across his resting place.

Papa's tomb was a large cement rectangle, painted white, that stood in the middle of the grave house. The grave marker had his name, the year he was born, and the year he died. He had been thirty-five years old. Carved beneath his name were my grandparents' names. Their bones had been buried in a special compartment under Papa's coffin. Sometimes, Mama and I had to hang our wash over the tomb to dry when it rained. It didn't seem like a nice thing to do, so we whispered, "Sorry, Papa," every time.

I pulled a key out of my shorts. It hung on a cord made

of tightly braided cloth. The small padlock on the gate was flimsy but it kept out other squatters. Mama bought one after a neighbor "borrowed" our broom while we were out and never gave it back. After pushing the gate open, I propped my rubber slippers at the bottom of the step and went inside, closing the gate behind me. Everything was just as I'd left it this morning. Stretched across Papa's tomb hung a string of sampaguita, a small, fragrant jasmine flower that filled the entire grave house with sweetness.

Mama and I slept on one side of the mausoleum. Propped against the wall were sheets of cardboard to cushion our backs from the concrete floor. There was also a basket that held a kulambo, or mosquito net, as well as a pair of thin blankets and pillows. Hidden inside the blanket was our only luxury, a flashlight. Mama always made sure the batteries were fresh. She said it was important to have, in case someone tried to come into our grave house at night. Other baskets held some clothes, mostly hand-me-downs, a small cracked mirror, a comb, and toothbrushes.

The other side of the tomb had a small plastic table we'd found at a trash heap and a woven mat where Mama and I sat to eat. Above the table hung a small wind chime made with three strands of capiz shells. They tinkled softly in the afternoon breeze. In the corner stood an altar made out of a small plastic crate I'd found behind a bakery, turned on its side. Mama had draped an old slip edged with lace over it. On top of the satiny cloth sat our Santo Niño, a statue of baby Jesus dressed in gold-and-red felt. It had a gold plastic crown on its head. It had been a gift from Papa's aunt, back when she was kind to us. At its feet lay a pile of small white sampaguita flowers I'd picked from a bush near the cemetery gates.

I pulled out the piece of candy Kuya Efren had given me and placed it in front of our Santo Niño. Papa used to come home from work with candy in his pocket for me. He'd let me eat only one and save the rest to make daily offerings to the statue. I'd asked him if baby Jesus took the sweets, because they disappeared every day. Now I knew better. Papa had eaten the candy when I wasn't looking. These days, Mama and I made offerings to our Santo Niño every time she went out to play mahjong, for blessings of both safety and luck. Then after a couple of days I would eat the candy, hoping for a never-be-hungry-again blessing.

Next to the gate stood a bucket I had found in a trash heap. Inside was a small sweet potato plant. At first, Mama wouldn't let me keep it inside the grave house. She had insisted that I keep it in the back, where we fetched water and did our washing. Then someone had stolen the sweet potatoes, and the leaves, which are also edible, before I had a chance to harvest them. After that, Mama let me keep it inside.

I pulled a sheet hanging from a stretch of wire across the bars. It was what we used when the season was dry. When it rained, we covered the bars with tarps that carpenters sometimes discarded after a construction job. I set my small bag of rice and fish on the table.

In the back of the grave house, behind the tomb, I pried open a loose tile that shielded my secret hiding place. Inside, covered with dust and spider webs, was an old shoebox. I emptied my pocket of coins and bills into it, my eyes straying to my father's watch and the picture inside the box. It was of me, Mama, and Papa, taken in front of our apartment several years before the fire destroyed our lives. Mama's cheeks were still round; her eyes looked bright and happy. She had long hair then and it draped thick over one shoulder. Papa was smiling big, his eyes disappearing into crinkles of skin. I was standing between them in my new school uniform, my hair in pigtails, ready for kindergarten. Papa had been so proud that day because I would be going to his old school, Joseph Luna Elementary School in Sampaloc, Manila.

I held the watch against my ear, listening to it count the seconds. It was almost like being a little girl again, when I used to press my ear to Papa's chest and listen to his heart. I kissed the watch face and turned the winding button three times.

The first time I held Papa's watch was during a surprise trip to Luneta Park. I had been a talkative kid and got in trouble a lot. When I saw Papa instead of Mama waiting for me after school, I wondered if he was there to talk to my teacher. But he smiled and took my hand.

"Why did you pick me up, Papa? Where's Mama?"

He kissed my forehead and said, "Remember Aling Lily from next door? Mama had to take her to the doctor, so she called me and asked if I could pick you up. So I thought, since I'm here, I can take you to Luneta Park like I promised."

"Really? Thank you, thank you, Papa!"

We rode a jeepney, a kind of jeep that's extra long in the back and works like a shared taxi. It can fit at least sixteen people, eight on each side. It took a long time to get to the park because of traffic. I fell asleep on Papa's shoulder for what seemed like seconds, and then Papa patted my cheek to wake me. We had arrived.

Papa explained that Luneta Park was also called Rizal Park. After we climbed out of the jeepney, I could see why. A monument to Philippine's national hero, Jose Rizal, stood at its entrance. Visitors and street vendors crowded the sidewalk; young people posed for pictures, while the old ones talked about Rizal's revolutionary novels to anyone who would listen.

We walked on the grassy lawn, weaving between families sitting on blankets. We stopped for ice cream and headed to a place called the "flower clock." It was a huge flower bed. The clock face was made of yellow and red flowers, with an actual hour hand and minute hand mounted in the center. I stood on a bench to get a better look. It really looked like a clock!

"Does it work?" I asked.

Papa shook his head. "I'm afraid not. Have you learned to tell time?"

I jumped off the bench and sat next to him. "Yes. Miss Lim gave us worksheets with clocks all over it so we can practice telling the time."

"Why don't we practice while we finish our ice cream. We can use my watch." He shook his wrist so that his watch faced me and pointed to it with his pinky. "Tell me, what time is it?"

I stared at it for a long time, not because I was trying to figure out what time it was, but because it was so pretty. It was silver all over, even the bracelet, but its face was blue. The hands ticking rhythmically were silver. "Can you tell me the story of your watch, Papa?"

"Again?" He laughed.

"Please?" I begged, swinging my legs as they dangled over the bench seat.

"Oh, all right." He smiled, squinting into the distance as if he could read the story from the sky. "This watch once belonged to your grandfather. When he was in college, he worked as a waiter for a popular restaurant in Manila called the Aristocrat. One day he was taking a break behind the building smoking a cigarette, when he heard someone shouting and witnessed a robbery. A thief had grabbed an old man's briefcase. The old guy wouldn't let go, so the thief kicked him. Your grandfather shouted for him to stop, just as the old guy fell to the ground. He chased the thief and wrestled the briefcase away from him. The thief ran away before your grandfather could call the police."

"And then what happened, Papa?" I had asked, licking the melted ice cream off my fingers.

Papa chuckled and continued, "He helped the old man up and returned his briefcase. The old man trembled and cried. Your grandfather could see that the old man needed to sit and rest to calm himself, so he invited him into the restaurant. The old man said he couldn't, he didn't have enough money, but your grandfather insisted. He brought the man inside and sat him at a corner table. The restaurant manager was a kind man and allowed your grandfather to bring the old man a cup of coffee, a small bowl of the restaurant's famous stew, dinuguan, and some fluffy steamed rice cakes. The old man told your grandfather he had been on his way to visit his wife, who lay dying in a nearby hospital. The briefcase contained love letters they had shared as young lovers and he'd brought them so he could read them to her. He finished his food, thanked your grandfather, and asked him for a glass of water. He went to fetch him the drink, but when he returned, the old man was gone. But on the table was a wristwatch sitting on top of a note written on a paper napkin."

Papa paused to eat his melted ice cream. "This is good!"

"Papa," I whined. "What did the note say?"

"Oh, yes," he continued. "The note said, 'Thank you for saving my memories. Please accept this small gift.' Your grandfather ran out of the restaurant to give the watch back to the old man. He looked up and down the street and could not find him. He even ran to the hospital where the old man said his wife lay dying, but the receptionist told him she hadn't seen an old man with a briefcase come in. While he was telling her the story, he noticed how lovely her eyes were, and how sweetly she smiled at him. That's how your grandfather met your grandmother. He wore the watch every day from then on to remind him of that special day. If it weren't for the old man and his watch, he wouldn't have met the love of his life."

I had always wondered what happened to the old man, and if his wife had noticed the tan line where his watch used to be. My grandfather had given the watch to Papa when he began going to college. One of his friends told him it was a vintage Seiko 5 Chronograph circa 1975. He'd loved his watch.

I loved it too. It was all Mama and I had left of Papa.

I placed the watch back inside the box and closed it. With the tile back in place, I picked up my basket and sat on my mat. My banig was bright pink with stripes of zig-zag yellow and blue. When we moved to the cemetery, Mama had decided we should have a colorful mat to sit on when we ate meals. She told me that we needed some brightness in our lives. I ran my fingers over the design, thinking about that, and realized she was right. It made me a little happy to look at it. I sighed, my thoughts straying to food. I wondered if Mama would bring home a steamed pork bun to share, or some fresh-baked pandesal with pats of butter wrapped in wax paper. Those would taste so much better than plain steamed rice and fried fish.

Ignoring my grumbling stomach, I shook out a bagful of dried gold and pink everlasting daisies. I began to work.

Chapter Two

I WOKE WITH A START, STILL SITTING ON MY WORKING mat, itching with mosquito bites. A pile of garlands lay beside me, dried everlasting daisies strung together with needle and thread. The bright yellow, orange, pink, and red flowers stood out against the dreary colors of the grave house. They would soon decorate altars in homes, or hang from rearview mirrors in jeepneys. I rubbed my aching eyes with sore fingertips. My candles had burned out, and my mat was littered with papery petals.

I tried to stay up and wait for Mama to come home. My neck ached. I rested my head against Papa's tomb. The cool cement felt good against the pounding in my temples.

It used to feel strange, knowing Papa was lying just

inside this cement block. I once asked if his ghost would visit us. The thought of it had frightened me. But Mama had shushed me. She'd said that his spirit had wandered the earth for forty days after he died but now he was in heaven. She also told me that Papa watched over us, and that his spirit would only appear if we wished it, and only in our dreams.

My hand absently pulled at the edge of my shorts as the pain in my head eased into a dull headache. The flattened cardboard box underneath my woven mat slid slightly on the cement floor. It reminded me of one of the things I missed the most. A real bed.

The gray light of morning filtered through the sheet covering the metal bars of my grave house, my cemetery home. All around me, the living slept among the dead. Some of them slept on mats or other makeshift beds. Others slept on top of tombs. They lived inside mausoleums with the few things they needed for daily life, like plastic dishes, basins, discarded furniture, and sometimes electric fans. They were squatters, like my mother and me, living in the Manila North Cemetery because it was better than living in the slums.

Where could Mama be?

I hated being alone in this miserable place. My chest ached for my old home, my old life. It felt like an impossible wish.

"Why didn't I ask her where she was going?" Papa could not hear me but it made me feel better to talk to him. At least he didn't talk back. Although sometimes I thought he did. Through my dreams. "I'm a stupid girl, Papa."

I'd waited all night for her to eat dinner with me. The bowls of rice and fish still sat on the small plastic table I'd salvaged from a trash heap. Both bowls were covered with plastic plates to keep out flies. The salty, pungent aroma of the fish drifted over to me, and my stomach grumbled. Should I eat now or wait for her? My stomach said "now." It also said to eat both bowls, and it would serve Mama right for making me wait.

My squatter neighbors were already up, either buying bread or fetching water. I could hear their slippers smacking the heels of their feet as they walked. Wooden pushcarts bumped and crunched over the cement outside. Someone stopped in front of my grave house. Relief washed over me like cool water over hot, dry skin. It was probably Mama. I shoved the bedsheet that covered the bars aside and called out, "Mama? Is that you?"

But it wasn't. It was Jojo, shirtless, wearing a loose pair of basketball shorts. His arms were twisted behind him, trying to scratch a spot in the middle of his back.

It had been hard for me to make friends. Many of the other squatter kids who had lived in the cemetery all their lives had stared at me suspiciously and then run away when I tried to talk to them. Not Jojo.

He was tall, and so thin that he reminded me of one those spiders with small bodies and long, skinny legs. His skin was darker than mine from all the time he spent in the sun. When he smiled, his wide nose flattened a little more. He had large black eyes and the longest, straightest eyelashes I'd ever seen on a thirteen-year-old boy.

He stood behind a cart made of pieces of scrap wood that held three large blue containers filled with water. The cart's wooden wheels were cracked and embedded with small rocks.

"Magandang umaga!" he said, grinning. "Well, you're up early."

His constant good humor was infectious. I sometimes forgot my sadness when he was around. "So are you. Are you making a delivery?"

"Siyempre! How do you think I earn my breakfast?" he said, and rubbed his stomach.

"Thanks for filling our water bucket yesterday. Your clothes should be dry by now." Jojo's and his grandmother's clothes were hanging on a line strung between an electrical pole and a nail on the grave house's wall. Squatters of the Manila North Cemetery helped each other out this way. Jojo filled a large plastic container behind my grave house with water for drinking and washing. Mama and I did laundry for him and his grandmother. It seemed a fair enough exchange to me.

"I'll pick it up later." He gave me a quick nod and pushed the heavy cart forward.

"Jo! Sandali lang!" He stopped and raised his eyebrow at

me. Heat surged into my cheeks, making them prickle uncomfortably. I wasn't sure I wanted to tell him that Mama hadn't come home last night.

"I was just wondering . . . my mother went to buy bread a little while ago. Have you seen her?"

He must've sensed something in my voice. His eyebrow crept up a little higher and disappeared into his choppy bangs.

"Hinde," he said, shaking his head from side to side. He leaned against the cart and stared at me. "She went to another one of those all-night mahjong games, didn't she?"

Did everyone know what Mama liked to do at night? "Actually, she . . ."

"Aha! She did, and she's probably still there mixing those mahjong tiles with bleary eyes." He stood there, pretending to mix invisible tiles on an invisible table with his eyes closed and drool dripping down his chin.

I stared at him and tried to smile. He always found a way to make me laugh, but I just didn't feel like it then.

He stopped and sighed. He stared down at his feet, frowning.

"I really hate it when she leaves you alone, Nora. You know I do! If you lived closer to me and my grandmother, then I wouldn't worry . . ."

"Yeah, I know. She'll be home soon, so you better get going or she'll accuse you of being a lazy bum." That wasn't true, of course. Mama loved him and always insisted that he stay and have breakfast with us.

Jojo shook his head as he turned to push his cart and said, "Sige, I better get going. I'll see you later."

"Well, if you see her, tell her I'm waiting for her." *And how much longer will that be?* I wondered. Mama and I had a washing job today. If she didn't show, I'd have to do it all, which meant it would take longer and the clothes wouldn't have enough time to dry. Then if I did a lousy job, we would get fired, which would mean eating only once a day instead of twice.

Jojo waved without looking back. I watched him go, wondering why I suddenly felt the urge to ask him to stay.

My stomach felt like a rubber band that was wound too tightly. Mama would be home soon. Maybe she'd dozed off at a friend's house or something. I just had to be patient.

If only she'd get here already.

The landscape of cement and granite tombs glowed in the pale morning light. I still couldn't believe that I really lived here now. Tombs were everywhere, as far as the eye could see. It looked like a small-scale city with avenues and streets. There were tombs with single walls, decorated with stone crosses and niches where you could place flowers. Some had houses built over them, like the one Mama and I lived in. Amid the tombs were the odds and ends of everyday squatter life. Shanties made of blue tarps, wood, and rusted corrugated metal sheets. Plastic buckets, basins, and rubber slippers positioned neatly in front of their entrances. One grave house had empty NIDO milk cans and RC Cola bottles stacked neatly inside a wooden cart. Rigged wires from electrical poles were spread out like spider webs, giving some squatters power for electric fans and small televisions. The squatters seemed content to call the cemetery home.

But not me and my mother. Not ever.

I kept my eyes on Jojo until he reached the end of the lane and turned onto the main street. The alley slowly came to life as the sun grew brighter in the sky. I watched for Mama while listening to the sounds of my neighbors. There was a mother scolding her child and a baby crying. Sounds of life among the dead.

My stomach finally drove me back inside to eat my share of the rice and fish, carefully wrapping Mama's bowl with a sheet of newspaper. I poured the leftover water from my glass over my sweet potato plant. The heart-shaped leaves were as big as my hands now. I slid the bucket close to the grave house door to catch as much sunlight as possible. After changing into clean shorts and a tank top, I hid my everlasting-daisy garlands inside a cardboard box. I left for the washing job with one question burning a hole the size of a coconut in my stomach.

Where are you, Mama?

Chapter Three

IT WAS BAD ENOUGH THAT MAMA WASN'T GOING TO show up, but now I was going to be late. She'd better not have made us lose this job too.

Mama and I worked as labanderas for Aling Lydia Ibarra, where we washed the family's clothes. This was the last of the laundry jobs we had, and we couldn't afford to lose it just because Mama had a gambling habit.

The sun was high and bright as I walked down the alley toward the cemetery gate. My neighbors were out and about, either waving a greeting or ignoring me. I was tempted to ask if any of them had seen Mama, but decided that it was pointless. Mama would be home and sleeping when I got back from work today. Maybe she'd win some money and would bring home something good to eat. I was getting tired of fried fish. The oily taste lingered in my mouth. Yuck. But then, it was better than having nothing to eat at all.

Once outside the gates, I wound my way down Bonifacio Avenue, past stands of flowers, candles, and snacks. I looked at the girls and boys who sat by their bouquets and roasted peanuts, calling out to customers as they walked by. Their job seemed easy when you compared it to washing clothes. Their hands were smooth, not dry and cracked like mine. If Mama and I could save enough money doing laundry and selling flowers, it would be nice to open our own stand. But the money went to mahjong, and whatever was left went to food and dried everlasting daisies. One of the vendors pulled out a cell phone and began typing out a text message. It was the kind that flipped open. Mama had one of those once. We only used it if we needed to call Tito Danny, my uncle, who lived on the island of Davao. You had to take a boat or a plane to get there. But now we couldn't call him anymore because Mama'd had to sell her phone.

A group of girls in school uniforms walked past me, carrying bags bulging with textbooks and notebooks. They were students from St. Anne's Academy, which was located down the street from the cemetery. It was a private school, which meant you couldn't go there unless you had money to pay for tuition fees. One of them caught me staring and rolled her eyes at me.

I had gone to a public school, where anyone could attend as long as you purchased your own uniforms and school supplies. Evelyn and I used to wear plain white blouses and maroon skirts, which were the standard uniforms at Joseph Luna Elementary. Now and then, I'd catch glimpses of students in the same colored skirts and wonder what Evelyn was doing, and if she remembered me. We used to talk about homework and shows on TV, the same way I heard those St. Anne's Academy girls do just now. Seeing them always made me long for those days again.

I sighed and crossed the street to Aling Lydia's home and business, the Ibarra Family Bakery.

The bakery stood on the corner of Andres Bonifacio Avenue and Basa Street. The early-morning crowd was gone but there were still customers buying their pandesal for breakfast. The smell of fresh-baked rolls always made my stomach grumble. I hoped Aling Lydia had set aside a few rolls for me today.

Her daughter, Perla, worked behind the counter alongside another girl. She usually helped out during the busy time in the morning before going to school. Perla, already dressed in her St. Anne's Academy school uniform, frowned at me as I passed. She was a girl about my age, with fair skin and pinkish cheeks and lips. Her nose was nice, with a high bridge and a small pointy tip. Unlike mine, which was wider, flatter. People in the neighborhood considered her quite a beauty.

"Well, it's about time!" called Perla as she looked down her nose at me, her arms crossed in front of her. "My PE uniform better be ready for tomorrow."

Once, I'd asked Mama why she was so bossy, and she'd told me to ignore it—that I had to play nice since Perla was Aling Lydia's daughter, and it was not my place to question her behavior. Perla had ignored me most of the time until a few weeks ago, when she'd seen me wearing one of her old Hello Kitty shirts. It turned out to be one of her favorites, and she hadn't known that her mother had given it to me, along with some of her other old things.

I didn't understand why she would be angry with me instead of her mother. I wanted to say something mean back to her but I needed to keep this job. All I could do was roll my eyes. I walked around the corner to their house. It was located right behind the bakery, separated by a paved courtyard that extended all the way to the back of the house. It was a two-story home with white cement walls, and windows covered with black iron bars that curled on the bottom like upside-down question marks. It had a raised front porch that faced the back door of the bakery, directly across the courtyard.

Aling Lydia sat on the front porch of her house holding a cigarette between manicured fingers, while counting out the clothes to be washed. She was a small woman, with a round face and a round body. Her short black hair formed a fuzzy halo around her heavily powdered face. She wore a duster with pink and yellow flowers, a loose cotton housedress that women wore at home.

Looking at her always gave me a little shock. Her face looked so pale against her black eyebrows and pink lips.

My own skin was so brown in comparison. Women like her, who remained at home with their maids or worked in nice jobs inside offices, were always careful about their complexions. They used umbrellas every day to protect themselves from the sun. When you were that fair-skinned, people tended to think you were someone special.

"Good morning, po."

Aling Lydia looked up, her brow arched high on her forehead. Then she smiled and gave me a nod. When she realized I was alone, she frowned, watching the street behind me to see if Mama would appear.

"Just you, Nora? Where is your mother?" She stood and pushed her cigarette into a flowerpot on the porch. It already had so many cigarette butts sticking out of the soil that they looked like mushrooms without their caps.

"She's sick today," I lied. In a way, Mama was sick. She had gambling-itis.

Aling Lydia shook her head, pressed her lips together, then let out a sigh. She gathered the clothes into her baskets. "I have six pairs of pants, five T-shirts, five blouses, three skirts, five dusters, and fifteen pairs of underwear. I also have towels from the house and aprons from the bakery, but since you're by yourself, those can be washed tomorrow. Do you think you can manage?" She stood there, eyebrows raised, waiting for an answer.

I hesitated, my fingers twisting the edge of my shirt. *I can do it.* I nodded.

"Well, the laundry has to be done. This is a lot of work for you to do on your own. If your mother fails to show up again, I may have to find another labandera, do you understand? I've been very patient with your mother. We are from the same town, after all, but that doesn't mean she can continue taking me for granted." She picked up the basket full of clothes and motioned for me to take the other one. Aling Lydia had a washing patio on the other side of the house. She set the basket of clothes down on the tiled floor. She had several plastic palangganas of different sizes. The basins were stacked by the wall, next to a faucet with a hose attached to it.

"The laundry soap is over there on the stool. It's a new bar, so don't use it all up. I'm going to the market now," said Aling Lydia, patting the sweat off her face. She softened her tone and said, "And if you get all of this done by the afternoon, I'll give you a nice treat along with the day's wages, okay?"

The *clap, clap, clap* of Aling Lydia's wooden slippers receded, then came back. "By the way, I found someone who wants to sell their manicure tool box. It comes complete with a supply of cuticle lotion, acetone, and a collection of nail polish. Let me know when you're ready to buy it." Then she walked away, humming to herself.

I had a hundred forty-five pesos in a little box hidden in the grave house along with Papa's watch. All I needed was another fifty-five pesos and I'd be able to pay Aling Lydia for the kit. I was so close. Doing manicures would make so much more money than selling everlasting-daisy garlands on street corners.

Looking at the pile of clothes made me think about

Mama again and where she could be. How could she do this to me? How could she leave me to do all this work on my own? I touched one of the pants and almost cried. Denim. It was so hard to wash by hand, because it was so heavy when it got wet. I kicked the stack of palangganas in front of me and pressed the heels of my hands over my eyes, willing myself to calm down and get to work.

I filled the largest basin with water and picked up the new bar of laundry soap. It was as long as my arm, and was actually four bars of soap stuck together. It was blue, with the letter T stamped on the surface of each bar. Mama had told me that bars were best for hand-washing. The stores sold laundry soap in bags of powder now, for people who had washing machines. I was glad Aling Lydia didn't have one of those. I broke off one bar and placed the rest on top of a stool where it would not get wet. I piled some of the clothes into the water and began scrubbing.

After we moved to the cemetery, Mama had taken me with her when she looked for washing work. I'd never washed clothes before but she said it was time for me to learn. She also told me if I worked alongside her, we could make enough money to move back to her family farm. We had been lucky and found three labandera jobs. She taught me how to soak the white clothes in a blue tint to prevent yellowing. She showed me how to squeeze water out of denim without hurting my hands, even though she only gave me the lighter pieces to scrub. We'd play little games while we rinsed the clothes, racing to see who would finish first.

I pushed those thoughts out of my mind. Remembering things like that only made me wish all the harder that Mama was here. Instead, I watched the bubbles form foamy hills and mountains in the basin as I scrubbed. I played a game with myself, counting how many pieces I could wash before the mountain of soapy fluff overflowed and oozed over the edge of the basin.

After an hour, I was emptying out the palanggana of soapy water, my arms covered with suds, when I heard the gate open. I could hear someone knocking on the front door, and then the sound of footsteps coming my way. The voices of two women grew louder as they drew closer.

"Tiger gives me the creeps! Did you see him leaning against the fence across the street?"

"You know, I heard that Lorna has been talking to him."

My heart nearly jumped out of my chest when I heard Mama's name. The palanggana almost fell out of my hands as I strained to listen.

"Oh, I knew that. But what I want to know is what they talk about. I bet it's nothing good. Anyway, Aling Lydia told me that if Lorna missed another day of work, she would have me take over. So that's why I'm here now. But it looks like Aling Lydia already left for the market."

"Come on, let's see if that good-for-nothing Lorna is there . . ."

Two women appeared around the corner of the house and stood looking at me with their mouths open like small black holes. One woman was very short, with gray hair pulled up into a knot on top of her head. The other woman was taller, about Mama's age, with black wavy hair that came down to her shoulders and a black mole with a hair growing out of it on her chin.

"Hey, what are you doing here?" said the smaller woman, a cigarette dangling from her lower lip.

"I work here, and you have no right to call my mother a 'good-for-nothing'!" I couldn't bring myself to say anything more. What right did they have to come here and think they could take Mama's job?

My job.

"Naku, of course she's not," mumbled the smaller woman, embarrassed. She dropped her cigarette to the ground and stepped on it. Then she nudged her friend, whose eyes traveled from the pile of clothes to me and then back again.

"Just tell Aling Lydia we came by," sneered the taller woman, and they turned to leave.

I slammed the bar of soap onto the concrete, breaking it in half. They were not going to take my job, no matter what happened.

I filled the empty basin with water for rinsing. I dunked the clothes one by one, my mind wandering back to those two women and what they had said. Who was that guy, Tiger? Why would my mother want to talk to him?

The questions pounded away at my head and there was nothing I could do to stop them.

Chapter Four

I WAS ELEVEN YEARS OLD WHEN WE MOVED TO THE cemetery, a few weeks after my home had burned to ashes. The news had called it the "Holy Week Fire" because it had happened a couple of days before Easter. It destroyed my whole neighborhood. I will never forget it. We lived in one of a row of small apartments located in Mandaluyong, a city that made up the eastern part of Metro Manila. It was a nice but poor neighborhood, full of life, where grownups worked in offices or as teachers, children went to school, and you could find a sari-sari store on every corner.

The fire had destroyed our small apartment with everything we owned and loved. When Papa died in the fire, time seemed to stop, and everything I saw seemed to have no color, no life.

Mama was strong and knew what needed to be done from the start. She had joined the long lines waiting for government money, and made sure we had a place near the bathrooms in the evacuation center set up in a local elementary school. When we received our relief money, we moved in with Papa's aunt.

Lola Fely, who insisted I call her Lola even though I really couldn't think of her as my grandaunt, had made all the arrangements to have Papa buried in their family crypt. She had arranged a weeklong vigil for Papa in her own home, since it would be too expensive to have a wake at a funeral home. Mama made sure all the donations she received during this time were given to Lola Fely to cover the expense of Papa's burial.

Afterward, Lola Fely welcomed Mama and me with open arms into her home. She lived with her son, along with his wife and three children. Her grandsons were older than me, all of them in high school. Mama and I slept in my cousin Elmer's room. He wasn't happy about it. Lola Fely had given us clothes, slippers, and towels. They weren't new, but we were thankful just the same.

Mama had been so grateful that she wanted to give some of our relief money to Lola Fely, who refused it at first, then accepted it after Mama insisted. I could tell by the way she kept sneaking a look at Mama that she only pretended she didn't want the money. Especially since she had arranged for a priest to come and say mass in honor of Papa's fortieth-day-of-death anniversary, the day his spirit would rise to heaven. She had paid for all the refreshments as well.

Mama expressed her gratitude by working alongside Lola Fely's maid, cleaning the house and washing their clothes. She also became the family cook. At first, Mama had wanted to move to Davao and live with her brother, who owned a farm. He had promised we could live in a hut he'd built himself near a grove of mango trees. But when Mama realized that we wouldn't be able to visit Papa's grave if we lived there, she changed her mind. She decided we should stay in Manila and she would look for a job. I sat by Mama when she told my grandaunt her decision. Lola Fely said it was fine, but I noticed how she pursed her lips, and it made me think she wasn't fine with it at all.

That's when the complaining started. Lola Fely would find spots on the floor that Mama didn't clean. She would whine to her son about how much she spent on food and water, making sure she said it loud enough so Mama could hear her from the kitchen. Mama pretended not to listen, but I saw a tear run down her cheek before she wiped it away. I felt my own eyes water and turned away so she wouldn't see. Lola Fely made comments about Mama's cooking at dinner. One night, she said Mama's adobo was too sour, and threw her spoon down on her plate, startling everyone. Mama apologized and left the table, embarrassed.

"Mama, let's go to Davao," I whispered to her as we

washed the dishes. I wanted to leave, to get away from Lola Fely, from Manila and all its painful memories.

Mama had sighed and shaken her head helplessly. "Once I find a job, it'll get better, you'll see. We just have to be patient."

It hadn't. Mama had made sinigang once, a delicious soup with tender pieces of pork and vegetables flavored with tamarind. My cousins deliberately ate most of the meat, leaving only a few vegetables for Mama and me.

Later that night, while we were getting ready for bed, Mama whispered, "I've been thinking—we still have money from Papa's savings and a little of the relief money left over to pay for bus and ferry tickets to Davao. Even if we can't visit Papa's grave, his spirit will be with us no matter where we are."

Mama told Lola Fely the next day.

"What? Why waste my nephew's savings on a boat ride? Why not put some of that money to good use and invest it in my dry-goods business? That way you can stay in Manila," Lola Fely had said. I could tell that Mama was too embarrassed to disagree.

The dry-goods store never came to be, and Lola Fely wouldn't acknowledge any questions Mama asked about her money. Instead, she bellyached about all her household expenses. She even complained about the wages she paid her only maid, Dina. Mama couldn't help herself and told Lola Fely that she was actually saving money, since she hadn't had to pay for a labandera since Mama and I had moved in.

Lola Fely had walked out of the room, her face red with anger.

Then one day, Lola Fely found me looking at Papa's watch after helping Mama sweep the front porch. It was the only thing of his that had been saved from the fire. I liked to keep it in my pocket so Papa would still be close to me in some small way.

"What do you have there? Your father's watch? Let me see it." She held her open palm out to me.

I looked at the outstretched hand and knew that if I handed over the watch, I would never see it again. I put the watch in my pocket and kept my eyes on the floor.

"You ungrateful child! You are shameless! How dare you keep that watch from me after all I have done for you and your mother? Did you know that she ruined your father's future?"

"What?"

She sneered like a snake about to swallow its prey. "That's right. Your father asked me not to tell, but he's dead now, so it doesn't matter. Your mother worked as a maid for our family and your father had the crazy notion he was in love. They eloped and broke your grandparents' hearts. In the end, it killed them both. That watch belonged to his father first, *my* brother. Now hand it over."

My eyes were glued to the floor, stung by the venom in her voice. My eyes filled with tears. *A maid?* It explained a lot. I'd always wondered why Mama treated Lola Fely with deference and even a little fear. I could see it in the way my cousins never invited me to go to the mall with them, and the way they made me sit on the floor when we watched television. I squashed the poison growing inside me. She wasn't going to make me hate my mother.

"You are a stubborn, stupid child, just like your father! Why do I bother . . ." Lola Fely continued to scream and brought my mother running from the kitchen. The whole house was in an uproar.

After that, I became invisible. Lola Fely wouldn't acknowledge me. She ignored me when I said "good morning" or if I asked her a question. Even my cousins didn't speak to me. When I'd come into the living room to watch cartoons with them, they'd turn off the television and leave the room.

When I told Mama about it, she became so angry. She told me Papa's other cousins weren't like Lola Fely's family at all. They were far kinder but couldn't afford to take us in. She said it was time to take action. She went to the market and bought a cell phone, the cheap kind that flipped open, with a small prepaid plan. Mama called her brother and asked for a loan to pay for bus and ferry tickets to Davao. But she told me Tito Danny said we had to wait at least six months so he could save enough money to send to us. She hugged me and told me to be strong, that six months wasn't very long.

But our welcome finally came to an end when Elmer accused me of stealing his cell phone. I had been dusting the living room when my foot tapped something under the coffee table. A cell phone slid into view. I picked it up. I knew it belonged to Elmer and was about to take it to him when the screen lit up. I paused, distracted by the messages, when Elmer walked into the living room.

"What are you doing with my cell phone? I've been looking for it since last night."

"I just found it under the coffee table. Here." I held the phone out to him.

He snatched it from me, rubbing the screen on his shirt. "You're a liar. I know I left it in my room yesterday. You stole it, didn't you?"

"No!" My voice cracked. I swallowed. "I told you. I found it here, just a few minutes ago!"

"Liar!"

Lola Fely walked in. "What's going on here?"

Elmer told her. Then his grandmother screamed at me. She said I was a good-for-nothing, an ingrate, a disappointment to my father. How dare I steal from *her* family. I cried and told her I hadn't done it, but she wouldn't listen.

She grabbed a broom, pointed the handle at me and yelled, "Dapa!"

Mama rushed into the living room in time to see me refusing to get on my hands and knees. Lola Fely handed my mother the broom and ordered her to beat me, and said if my mother didn't, she certainly would.

Mama couldn't take it anymore. She grabbed me by the arm and dragged me up the stairs, into our room. She calmed me down and told me she believed me.

We packed up our few possessions, waited until morning, and left. I had no idea where we were going. Were we going to live in the streets? Then Mama told me we were moving to the cemetery. She said that Papa's family mausoleum at least had a roof and ample space for sleeping. *Sleeping?* Before I could say a word, Mama reassured me that we were not going to be the only ones there. She had meant the living, not the dead.

Squatters lived there, a fact I had never noticed at Papa's funeral. But would it be better than living under Lola Fely's grinding heel and accusing eyes? At the time, I'd tried to cheer myself up with the thought that at least we would be close to Papa.

In order to survive, my mother and I took laundry jobs from households outside the cemetery gates. I could not go to school, since we couldn't afford to replace the uniforms I had lost in the fire or buy school supplies. The work gave us sore backs and dry, raw hands, but we were getting paid for it. It wasn't a lot of money, just enough for food and other needs like soap and candles.

Our grave house was the last one in a long row of mausoleums at the end of an alley. Lola Fely was content enough to let us live here, since she wouldn't have to pay a caretaker to keep the mausoleum clean, the grave markers dusted and polished. Especially for All Saints' Day, when relatives would come to visit. When that happened, Mama and I had to move out all of our belongings and hide.

Most of the grave houses in my alley had people living in them. One of them had a cradle made of palm leaves suspended with rope from the ceiling. Someone even had kerosene lamps and a radio. It had been scary to live here at first, but Mama told me that the living would do us greater harm than the dead ever could.

I believed her.

Chapter Five

On the way home, I stopped at a flower stand and bought a bagful of dried everlasting daisies to string into garlands later. It bounced against the other bag I carried. Aling Lydia had given me some bread, cheese, and steamed pork buns. I wanted to pull one out and eat it right there in the street but I decided to wait and share it with Mama. She was probably there by now.

I ran the rest of the way home.

The plastic bags I carried swung on my arm like pendulums. I dodged people buying flowers and candles at the gate, passed a funeral march down the main cemetery street, and jogged around some small children playing a game of hopscotch. The money Aling Lydia had paid me was pinned inside the pocket in my waistband. The bulkiness of the pouch was comforting against my stomach. She'd paid me only half of the usual fee because the other half of the laundry would be done tomorrow. If I could sneak a little of the money into my hiding place, then my puhunan would be almost complete.

I hoped Mama would stay home tonight. I could tell her about that gossiping woman who wanted to steal her job. That would make her want to go to work tomorrow. Then we would eat the pork buns for dinner and maybe go to a neighbor's grave house and watch a show on her small television. A mausoleum painted sky blue marked the entrance to our alley. It was larger than my grave house, with barred windows on two sides, as well as a gated front entrance. There were two tombs inside. Little Ernie and a couple of his friends were usually perched on top of one of them playing cards, but now there was no one there.

That was strange. There were always people hanging around. Tina, a young mother who lived in the grave house next to mine, liked to sit outside watching her baby walk and play with the other kids. Another neighbor was usually roasting corn on chicken wire, set over hot coals inside a large can that used to contain powdered milk. The can of coals was there, thin gray smoke curling above it, but there was no one around.

Little Ernie came out of Aling Nena's place and walked toward me. He seemed nervous. Strange. He kept looking over his shoulder at the empty alley.

"Hi, Ernie."

He motioned frantically for me to be quiet and tried to push me back in the direction of the main road.

"What's the matter?"

"Don't go home yet. Wait here until I get back, okay?" Ernie whispered. Then he ran down the main road and out of sight before I could ask him why.

What in the world was that all about? My stomach twisted and the hairs on my arms were standing on end when I noticed Aling Nena's and Tina's grave houses with sheets pulled across the bars. It was as if they were hiding. But from what?

A voice I didn't recognize drifted toward me from the end of the alley. As my feet took me closer, I could distinguish two, maybe three voices. My heart began to pound when I realized the voices were coming from *my* grave house.

"You pig! Will you stop eating and keep a lookout?"

"In a minute. And don't call me a pig, you bug-eyed monkey."

"Now you're really asking for it."

"Stop it! Or I'll kick both your . . ."

"Hey, boss! Look at this."

The loud clang and crash of a broken tile echoed down the alley. I quickened my pace and hid behind the wall of the grave house next to mine. My heart pounded so loud, I was afraid they'd hear it.

Oh, no—they found my hiding place.

I had discovered the hole when I'd crawled around the

tomb to retrieve a coin that had rolled behind it. When the tile shifted, I was sure I'd broken it, and thought Lola Fely would find out and punish me.

There had been candles inside the hollow space, covered in a blanket of dust and cobwebs so thick you couldn't tell what color the candles were. There was also a box of matches. I'd left the candles out and decided to use the hole to hide my old shoebox containing Papa's watch, the picture, and later on, money. Mama never questioned where the candles came from, and as far as I knew, she didn't know about that hole behind the tomb.

And now someone else had found it.

I held my breath and peered into my grave house. My knees trembled and would've given out if I hadn't been clutching the cement wall.

The black bars of the gate stood open. There was nothing left of the small padlock except for the U-shaped piece still hanging from it. The rest lay in pieces on the cement below.

Littered over the floor were the contents of our baskets. My sweet potato plant had been knocked over, dirt scattered in a halo around it. Some of its leaves had been trampled. Clothes, towels, and underwear were being kicked around by three of the ugliest men I had ever seen.

One of them was short and squat, his brown knobby knees so bowed that he rocked from side to side as he walked and pushed my things all over the floor. The second one was tall and thin, like a stick man. He paced the grave house, his bulging eyes fixed on the guy sitting on top of Papa's tomb while he finished off the rice and fish I'd left for Mama.

A sudden rush of anger filled my head. My temples felt like someone was pushing their fingers against them, trying to get through to my brain. The one sitting on Papa's tomb must be the leader. How dare he sit there like some kind of king! In his lap was the old shoebox I had hidden in the floor behind the tomb.

If fear made me a coward, then anger made me careless. I rushed at the one that was holding my box. I wanted to pull him off the crypt, but the skinny one grabbed me by the arms and pulled me back.

"Hey! Get off my father's tomb!"

The guy raised his eyes slowly, and then stared at me long and hard.

"You must be Nora. Your mother told me about you."

My skin tingled with a chill, even though the air was hot and still. Words like "So what?!" and "Who do you think you are?" got stuck in my throat. Fear was like glue; it sealed my mouth shut. My stomach churned at the thought that someone, this stranger, knew who I was. What was Mama doing, talking to someone like him?

"Hey, Tiger! What do you want me to do with her?" asked the skinny guy. Panic rose in my throat like vomit.

Tiger. This had to be the guy those gossips were talking about. He had pale patches of skin on his otherwise dark face. His hooded lids hung over eyes with yellowish whites, and his lips were both purple and brown at the same time.

His thin, sticklike body reminded me of a mosquito, with cheekbones and a chin that stuck out at sharp angles. He held a cigarette between his bony fingers. A flash of silver and blue caught my eye as the stranger raised the cigarette to his lips.

Papa's watch.

No.

"Take that off! And let me go, you cockroach!" I tried to pull my arm away, twisting and kicking at his shins, but the thug wouldn't let go.

Tiger held up his arm for me to see, and smiled. He was missing a few of his bottom teeth. "It looks good on me, ha? Don't worry, I'll take good care of it," he said. The watch slid up and down on his bony wrist, the silver bracelet too big for him.

My face felt hot. My hands knotted into fists. I wanted to claw those yellow eyes out. "Don't take my father's watch! If my mother owes you money, I'll pay it back. Just let me have my father's watch. Please."

"Actually, she owes my boss money. She's late with her payments, so I'll hold on to this as collateral," he said. He placed the cigarette between his lips, and smoke drifted out of his nose. "I'm not here to talk about your mother's debts. Like I said, your mother told me a little about you, and I was . . . well . . . curious."

His words made me cringe.

Who was his boss? Jojo had told me once that there were people who lent money out and expected to be paid back with interest. I think he called them loan sharks.

No. Mama would never borrow money from someone like that.

"You're lying." My voice shook, as if I didn't believe what I'd just said. Was this the reason why Mama had talked to this guy? There had been a moment here and there, when I'd wondered where Mama had found the money to continue playing mahjong. She had said once that she sometimes won big in the beginning and instead of stopping, she'd go on playing, only to lose it all again. I didn't think she'd borrow money just to gamble it away. I stood up straighter. "It's not true. She wouldn't borrow money from you or your boss."

"I don't care if you believe me or not. I know it's true, and so does your mother."

Tiger slid off the tomb and stood in front of me. I tried to back away, but the skinny one held me in place. Then Tiger walked around in a circle, studying me.

"There's a way for you to help pay your mother's debt. You can join my gang of pickpockets. I'll give you good food to eat, and even some money. Why don't you come with us?" He stepped closer. His breath smelled like an overflowing ashtray.

I finally twisted out of the skinny man's grasp and ran to the door. "I'm not going anywhere with you. Give me back my father's watch, or . . . or . . ."

"I don't think so," said Tiger. He sauntered past me. "Come on, boys. There's nothing left for us here. Think about our offer, Nora."

Before I knew what I was doing, I grabbed his wrist. "Give me back the watch!"

He pulled my hair with his free hand and yanked my head back. I screamed. He twisted his other hand out of my grasp and clamped it over my mouth, pushing me back against the wrought-iron bars of the grave house.

I clawed at his hand, forcing my fingers between his palm and my face. When he looked over his shoulder and nodded to his friends, his grip loosened for a moment. I opened my mouth, pressed his fingers against my teeth, and bit down with all my strength.

"Aray!" He whipped his hand away and jumped back. He hissed as he stared at his finger, blood seeping out of the cuts my teeth had made. "You think this little bite is gonna stop me?" He started to walk toward me and froze. There were shouts coming from up the alley.

"Nora!" Jojo's familiar voice almost made me faint with relief.

With one last angry look at me, Tiger and his gang ran out and away from the approaching voices.

"Alis! Go back to the rats on your side of the cemetery, you piece of trash!" yelled a wiry, toothless man wearing a red baseball cap. He ran past my grave house carrying a big stick. Jojo and another young man followed close behind him.

It was Aling Nena's husband, Mang Rudy, and their son Virgil. Mang Rudy was a carpenter and stonemason by trade. Virgil drove a motorcycle with a sidecar called a tricycle. They made it their business to keep our alley safe from thugs like Tiger.

"Nora, are you all right?" Jojo's eyes were wide and pleading, his eyebrows arched so high that they had disappeared beneath his bangs. If I hadn't been scared to death, I'd have laughed.

My throat ached and my knees buckled beneath me. Jojo caught me by the arms before I hit the floor. He held me up until I could stand again.

"Don't let me catch you around here again or I'll call the police!" Mang Rudy yelled, pulling his cell phone out and flipping it open to show he was serious. Tina, her baby on her hip, Aling Nena, and Ernie stood out in the alley, their eyes fixed on me. It made me want to run and hide. My cheeks felt hot. Why did they have to stare at me? I tried not to look at them. I didn't want to see the pity in their eyes.

"What happened here?" asked Mang Rudy. He didn't wait for me to answer. "What were those good-for-nothing roaches doing in your grave house? Were they meeting your mother here? Don't look at me like that. I've got ears and I know your mother is friendly with that piece of trash."

"But . . . but . . ." He was right, of course. Mama's gambling had really gotten out of hand. Now she was borrowing money from a loan shark. My eyes blurred, and Mang Rudy's face went in and out of focus as he continued to lecture me on being careful whom I associated with. That it was wrong for my mother to be on friendly terms with the likes of Tiger and that we should both have the common sense to stay away from him. What I didn't understand was, why was I getting lumped in with Mama? I wanted to say so, but my mouth stayed closed, my lips pressed together so hard my jaw ached.

Mang Rudy paused his scolding and looked around my grave house. His eyes traveled over the mess, his forehead furrowed. "Well, it's late. Where's your mother?"

"She'll be home soon." My voice was so soft that he leaned closer and made me repeat what I had said. I couldn't look him in the eyes. He might notice the doubt and worry that filled my own.

"Well, I hope you're right. Don't forget what I told you, ha?" He clamped his hand on my shoulder and gave it a shake. Then he turned to walk home with Virgil, who was standing in the alley talking quietly with Jojo.

"Salamat po." My voice came out barely above a whisper. They turned and waved to me, and gave Jojo a thumbs-up.

Jojo looked at my face and said, "I ran into little Ernie and he told me that Tiger was here. We ran to get Mang Rudy and Virgil. It looks like we got here just in time. Are you sure you're okay?"

I gazed, numb inside, at the clothes strewn on the floor and at the bruised leaves of my sweet potato plant.

"Yeah, I guess so." I wiped away the tears on my cheeks. "Let's go get your laundry before it gets too dark."

But I wasn't okay. I wouldn't be okay until I got Papa's watch back . . . and until Mama told me the truth.

Chapter Six

I REMEMBERED THE DAY MAMA AND I MOVED TO THE cemetery. We had left Lola Fely's home before everyone woke up. All we had were our baskets, a mat, a broom, and a couple of buckets.

Mama had a little money left and used some of it to hire a tricycle to take our things to the cemetery. On the way there, we stopped at the street market, or palengke. Mama bought some cheap plastic bowls and glasses, along with a few spoons, forks, and a knife. She seemed almost happy, now that we were away from Lola Fely's house. I would be, too, if I didn't think too hard about where we were going to live.

On the way out, I noticed a place that sold furniture and

lamps made from wicker, bamboo, dried palm leaf, and capiz shells. I trailed behind my mother, my steps growing slower, and before I knew it, I was inside the store. My fingers trailed over the pink, yellow, and blue pattern of a woven mat, and then through strings of pearly, translucent capiz shells hanging from wind chimes of all sizes. Papa had once told me about how, as a boy, he and his brothers would help his uncle collect baskets of windowpane oysters, which is what capiz is made of. He once helped me make a small wind chime out of these shells for a school project.

"Nora!" Mama stood at the store's entrance, breathing hard. "I thought you were right behind me."

"Oh, sorry, Mama. Look at this. It's just like the one Papa helped me make for school a couple of years ago. Remember?"

Mama's eyes shifted to the wind chime I had been looking at. The lines in her forehead softened as she drew near. The corners of her mouth lifted. She reached out a hand and brushed the strands of shells, listening as they tinkled.

"I wish we could buy it," I whispered. I knew we didn't have a lot of money.

Mama looked at me, then at the wind chime. She pressed her lips and nodded. "Let's do it. We'll buy another mat too. Something nice to sit on while we eat."

"But Mama—" She pressed a finger to her lips and signaled for me to keep quiet.

I watched Mama haggle with the vendor and then hand

him her payment for both items. On our way out of the market, Mama noticed my frown. She told me not to worry, that we would make that money back easily.

We had arrived in the cemetery late in the morning. The squatters who lived in the mausoleums nearby watched us without trying to look obvious. Mama paid the tricycle driver a little more than he had asked for, and he helped us unload our things. She always said it was good to be generous so that generosity would be shown to us in turn.

We opened the gate to the mausoleum and looked around. I hung the wind chime from a hook in the ceiling. The strands of capiz tinkled, then grew still. From out of her canvas bag, Mama pulled out two small candles, matches, and a framed picture of Papa as a young man. I recognized the photo that had hung in Lola Fely's living room and gasped. Mama smiled. She held a finger across her lips to stop the question I was about to ask. She propped the picture next to Papa's grave marker, placed the candles on either side, and lit each one.

Mama and I prayed for Papa to watch over us while we lived here. Afterward, we stood up, brushing dust off our knees. She reached for her walis tingting, a handleless broom made of the dried ribs of the coconut leaf, and began sweeping the floor along the base of the tomb.

"Nora, why don't you fetch some water so we can wash the dust off the floor."

I remembered seeing a faucet somewhere along the main road with a garden hose attached to it and headed over there with the buckets. I filled them both to the brim. I was halfway to the grave house when I heard someone say, "You're leaving a trail."

I turned to look and saw that I was, in fact, leaving a trail of water behind me. That was when I saw Jojo for the first time. He was sitting on a tomb by the side of the road with his legs folded beneath him, a wide grin on his face.

I ignored him and kept walking. My arms and hands burned from the weight of the buckets. Who knew that water could be so heavy!

"You're gonna spill half your water by the time you get home." He jumped off the tomb and jogged over to stand in front of me. He tried to help by taking one of the buckets.

"Hey!" I swung the bucket away, sloshing more water out. "What makes you think I live here?"

"Why would you need to fetch water if you don't live here? Hmm?"

"Hmmmp!" He was right but I wasn't about to admit it. I tried to move past him but he blocked my way. I eased the buckets down, trying not to spill any more water. I had to put them down anyway because my fingers were beginning to feel numb. When he reached for the buckets again, I smacked his hands away.

"Come on, I'm trying to help. I'm not gonna steal your buckets, if that's what you're worried about. By the way, my name's Jojo."

I pretended I hadn't heard his name. "I can manage just fine, thank you."

"Hey, aren't you going to tell me your name?"

I rolled my eyes and bent to pick up the buckets. Jojo grabbed one of the handles and said, "I'll carry this one, and if you can carry that other bucket without spilling any more water, then you won't have to tell me your name, okay?"

He grinned at me, proudly displaying the gap between his two front teeth. He picked up the bucket and started off in the direction of my grave house. He must've been watching me for a while. He walked in a loping gait with his other arm stretched out for, what? Balance? The water surface in the bucket remained glassy and still as he walked.

Hmp! If he could do it, then I could as well. I imitated his posture and his walk, and followed him. By the time I got to my new "home," my shorts were wet and my toes were squishing and squeaking in my wet rubber slippers. Mama was standing outside the grave house, smiling broadly, as Jojo spoke and pointed to different parts of the cemetery. They both turned when I set the bucket down. Jojo's eyes twinkled with mischief.

Mama slapped her hands together and said, "There she is! I was just talking to your new friend. Oh, good, you have the other bucket with most of the water still in it. See, Jojo"—she turned to face him—"I told you she could do it."

If my eyes could shoot fire, Jojo would have turned into charcoal.

"He isn't my friend." My teeth were clenched so hard I could barely get my words out. Who did this boy think he was? And why was he so at ease in a place like this? I thought I would see my misery mirrored in the faces of other squatters, but not this guy.

Mama paid no attention to my mumbling and told me Jojo would take us to meet his grandmother. He was also going to help us gather some of the supplies we needed to make our grave house livable.

Not only did I have to tell him my name, but he became a fixture in my life here in the cemetery. He always came by when he had nothing to do. Jojo had grown on me, but I couldn't bring myself to open up to him. It would have been nice to have a friend to talk to, someone other than Mama. I missed Evelyn the most during these times. Jojo was nice, but he couldn't be the kind of friend Evelyn had been to me. Besides, keeping him close would only hurt me in the end. Something would happen and I would lose him the way I'd lost Evelyn. Despite it all, I was glad to have him around.

Especially now, after Tiger had taken my father's watch.

"So . . . are you going to tell me what happened?" Jojo leaned back on his hands, his legs stretched out over the mat we were sitting on. He was wearing a T-shirt now, with the sleeves rolled up almost to his shoulders. A small pile of clothes lay between us, a combination of Jojo's and his grandmother's, all folded and ready to go.

"Your lola has pretty dusters." The cotton housedress on top of the stack was old, with faded blue flowers on a background of lemon yellow. I smoothed out the last wrinkle, picked up the pile, and held it out to him.

He didn't move to take it from me. He just sat there with an expectant look on his face, wriggling his foot. Oh boy, he was in full "big brother" mode now.

"Well, you saw what happened," I said, sighing. The grave house didn't look as messy as it had earlier. Jojo had helped me clean up, which consisted mostly of throwing things into the empty baskets and setting them aside for tidying up later on. They were lined up against the wall like garbage to be thrown out. I scooped the soil back into my sweet potato plant, patting it down to keep the stems from drooping. Mama's Santo Niño altar had been left alone, thank goodness. I had swept the floor and rolled out my pink and yellow mat to sit on.

"What in the world did they want? Is it true that your mother made a deal with Tiger?" asked Jojo. He stretched his leg out and pulled the plastic bag of food off the table using his toes.

I smacked his leg in disgust. His foot hit the table and jostled a bucket full of water that stood next to it, knocking the cardboard cover off. The water sloshed out and ran down its side, forming a small puddle beneath it.

Jojo rubbed his calf. "Aww, see what you did? Anyway, don't you pay any attention to who your mother hangs out with?"

"How was I supposed to know?" My throat tightened at

the hurt look on his face. I wasn't being fair to him. I wanted to talk to him, but I didn't know how to begin. He'd been nothing but nice to me since the first time I met him.

With an exhausted sigh, I opened the plastic bag from Aling Lydia. We talked about what I'd heard from the gossips earlier in the day and what Tiger had said to me about my mother.

"I didn't even know who Tiger was until today." The shoebox I kept Papa's watch in lay empty beside me. Even the money I had saved was gone.

"He's bad news, that guy," Jojo said through a mouthful of steamed pork bun. "He and his little gang live over in the Chinese cemetery. You know, he killed my best friend a couple of years ago. Tiger tried to take my friend's money but he resisted. That bastard beat him up so bad—we got him to the hospital but he died anyway. Teddy was on his way to buy medicine for his father. I was supposed to go with him. Boy, was my grandmother glad I didn't." He swallowed, his eyes focused on the past for a moment. "I wish I had gone with him, though. I would've made him give Tiger the money."

Then he sighed, grabbed a pandesal, and bit into it. "Hey, I heard that Tiger works for some businessman now, if you can believe that. He takes care of the family tomb or something."

"How awful for you and Teddy's family. But why would my mother have anything to do with him at all?" It had to be because of the gambling, but I didn't want to believe it. Why would Mama take that risk? She'd never mentioned the idea of borrowing money at all. I couldn't finish the pork bun in my hand. I had taken only one bite, but it felt stuck in my throat, as if I had swallowed the whole thing. Plus, my lips felt bruised, swollen. I squeezed my eyes shut, blocking out the memory of Tiger's filthy hand covering my mouth.

Jojo shook his head and frowned. "Who knows? But if he comes back here again, he'll be introduced to my balisong dance. I'm not losing another friend to that dog!" He jumped to his feet and slashed the air with an invisible knife. "Check it out, Nora. All you have to do is slash across like this and they'll leave you alone. I had a neighbor that taught me . . . Hey, are you okay?" asked Jojo. He peered into my face.

"Yeah, I'm okay. It's just that . . ." I swallowed the lump in my throat. "It's getting dark and Mama hasn't been home since last night. She's always home by now."

"I have an idea. Why don't you stay with my lola and me till your mother comes home? I can ask little Ernie to come and get you when she shows up."

It sounded like a good idea. I wouldn't have to be alone, even though I was sure that Mang Rudy, and the whole alley for that matter, were on the alert. Tiger wouldn't, shouldn't come back if he knew what was good for him. And Jojo's lola was nice. But it was still hard for me to accept this sort of help, and not feel that someday the same person who helped you would be the same one to hurt you later on. Just like Lola Fely. I just couldn't go through that again.

"No, that's okay. I'll just stay here and wait for her. She'll be home any moment now, you'll see." I held out the stack of folded clothes to him.

He raised his hand for me to wait. He tore a strip of cardboard from the flattened box Mama and I used as padding under our sleeping mat. Jojo folded the strip and showed me how to jam it between the gate hinges to keep it from opening.

"That should do it until you buy another padlock. Those thugs would be idiots if they try to come back here. Still, I want you to feel safe," he said, taking the pile of clothes from me. He stuffed another bun in his mouth and strode away. "Thanks for this and the snack. Goodnight."

I closed the gate and shoved the folded cardboard where Jojo had instructed me to. It worked. When I unhooked the bedsheet to draw it across the bars, I noticed Jojo walking back.

"Take this and keep it near you, just in case," he whispered, looking up and down the alley. He reached through the bars, placed something in my hand, and walked away. It was made of wood, scarred and worn from use. I turned it over in my hands and saw that it was made of two rectangular pieces stuck together on the long edge. I pulled them apart and out of its center came a shiny thin blade. I looked after Jojo in wonder. It was a butterfly knife, his balisong.

Chapter Seven

MY KULAMBO LOOKED LIKE A HOVERING GHOST IN THE flickering candlelight. Its corners were tied to loops of rope Mama and I had attached to the ceiling. Its gauzy material covered my sleeping mat in order to keep mosquitoes out. I crawled into it, leaving the candle burning in the corner. Being inside my kulambo felt safe. The netting blurred my surroundings, helping me forget where I was, even for just a while. The balisong lay on the mat beside me. I folded my arm under my head and lay there, watching the candlelight flicker on the knife's polished handle. I waited for Mama, too confused and exhausted to sleep.

Mama hadn't always been this way.

After she had learned to play mahjong Mama began

organizing a few of the neighbors to come over and play. Mama did this once a week, usually on a Wednesday, before she had to pick me up from school. Sometimes, instead of mahjong, they would play bingo. She was always in a good mood on that day. Papa had said he was glad Mama and her friends had a good time, as long as they only played for snack money.

I began looking forward to Wednesday afternoons because Mama would take me to her favorite turo-turo, a stand that sold a variety of sweet and savory dishes.

"What do you feel like having today, Nora?" she'd ask, peering at the pans of hot food behind a glass case.

"I want some ginataan," I'd say, bouncing on my heels.

Mama always ordered the same thing I did. We'd sit outside at a small table covered with red-and-white checkered plastic, blowing into small Styrofoam bowls full of my favorite snack. It was made of cooked sweet potatoes, saba bananas, taro root, jackfruit, and sticky rice balls in a sweet coconut cream sauce.

Afterward, we would go to the market so I could buy stickers for my notebooks, and Mama would buy mangoes to eat after dinner. It was Papa's favorite fruit.

When we moved to the cemetery, I had believed that Mama played mahjong because it gave her comfort, reminding her of Papa and our Wednesday afternoons together.

"I'll win big tonight, Nora. You'll see," she always said before going to an all-night mahjong game. And for a while, I had the same hopes. I wanted to get out of the cemetery someday and live in a real house.

Whenever Mama came back from a game with her purse empty, I began to realize that winning big wasn't going to happen easily. Mama never saw it that way, though. She wanted to win badly and thought of nothing else. There wasn't a game she wouldn't try. She even bought lottery tickets. Once, she lined up at a television studio for an entire day to watch a TV game show called *Wowowee* where they selected people from the audience to play games and win money. She never got in.

Then Mama started playing mahjong at wakes held at funeral homes outside the cemetery. At first, she would go only once a week, on Saturday afternoons. She took me with her once, but I complained so much about being bored, I broke her concentration on the game and she lost. I was considered bad luck after that. Instead, I would work on math or reading exercises Kuya Efren gave me. Sometimes, I'd hang out with our next-door neighbor, Tina, and play with her baby until Mama came home.

After a few months, Mama also started playing on Friday nights. She would come home very late. Then she'd go back and play all day Saturday. And Sunday. She would be too tired to work the next day. She'd even find a reason to play during the week. I would try to stop her but she'd always promise it would be her "last time." She broke her promises. We used to wash clothes for three different households. Mama would either make us late for the job or she'd make a mistake, like accidentally bleaching a pair of jeans. We had lost two of those jobs, no matter how hard I tried to cover for her.

Most of the time, she lost all the money she brought with her to the mahjong game, which was usually half of whatever we made on a washing job. She would come home at dawn, irritated, muttering to herself as she crawled under the kulambo to lie down. I'd keep my back to her and pretend to be asleep, relieved that she had finally come home.

There were times when she did win, but it wasn't what I would consider winning big. Instead of saving it Mama would go out and spend it on silly things, like a fancy pair of sequined Bombay slippers for herself, or a plastic Hello Kitty coin purse for me.

"I have to look decent enough so they'll let me play, you know," she'd say as she admired the new pink cotton dress she also bought with her winnings. I'd frown and tell her it looked expensive. Then she'd distract me with stories about Davao, and what it was like to grow up there. How wonderful the farm was, how many carabaos her brother, Danny, had. She'd promise to write to him, so he could send money or come to Manila to take us home.

I'd listen and get carried away, daydreaming about Tito Danny's farm and the fresh food we would eat. It made my mouth water to think about eating eggs and pandesal with cheese made from water-buffalo milk. We had to save at least five thousand pesos to get there by boat. We couldn't save even five hundred pesos.

That was when I decided to do whatever I could to make and save money. Replanting my sweet potatoes every time I harvested was one way. Mixing boiled sweet potatoes with cooked rice expanded one meal into two. Since I was down to only one washing job, I spent my free days selling everlasting-daisy garlands at the cemetery gates to visitors, who hung them on statues of saints or on altars at home. The little I made went to my savings. I wanted to buy supplies and do home manicures and pedicures. One of my squatter neighbors did it, and she made almost ten times more money than I did selling the garlands.

With that much money, I could buy those boat tickets. Mama and I would live with Tito Danny and his family and I could go back to school.

Maybe.

Late yesterday morning, Mama had been up and dressed in her pink cotton dress and Bombay slippers when I came home to pick up more daisy garlands. There were lots of people visiting the cemetery and I'd sold twenty of them in just a couple of hours. She held out her hand to me as if waiting for something.

"How much money have you made? Come on, where is it?"

"From a washing job? It's Saturday, Mama, there's no work today," I said, pretending not to know what she really wanted.

She stared up at the ceiling. "I meant the money you made selling everlasting-daisy necklaces. Come on, split it with me!"

I ignored her outstretched hand and pulled a neatly bundled set of daisy garlands out of a box. I hung them over my arm. Mama stood in front of my only exit.

"Anak, don't I share everything with you? Didn't I buy you a new pair of slippers? Come on, this could be my lucky night!"

She had bought me new ones. But now my slippers had a small hole right under the heel. She was making it really hard for me to stick with my plan. "Ma, you know I'm saving this money so I can buy my manicure tool case. Aling Lydia said she would help me."

"But you've never given a manicure. Who will teach you? Not me, I've never given one and probably never will."

"Tina will teach me. She used to give manicures before she sold her kit after having her baby. She'd said she'd introduce me to some of her former clients. If I do home manicures and pedicures, I'd make double, even triple of what I make now selling garlands. At least I'm not throwing money away." *Like you are,* I almost said.

Mama pursed her mouth; her face became sad and thoughtful. Her cheeks looked hollow, and the bones on her shoulders stuck out so much that they showed through the neckline of her dress. She looked away just when I saw a tear form at the corner of her eye.

I sighed and undid the safety pin to take money from a

pocket sewn into the waistband of the shorts I had been wearing yesterday.

"No, keep it," whispered Mama. She looked up at me, her mouth set in a determined line. "There's someone I have to talk to. I'll be back as soon as I can, okay?"

She came to me, held my face between her rough hands, and kissed me on the forehead. Then she'd left.

Now, I stared at the candle flame with the same dread I'd had when I watched her leave yesterday. I hadn't asked her where she was going.

Now I wished I had.

Chapter Eight

I AM HUDDLED IN THE CORNER OF MY ROOM, CLUTCHING my pillow to my chest. Smoke is snaking in under my bedroom door, rising to the ceiling, filling the air. The windows are covered with bars. There is no way out. I can hear my father shouting.

It's hot, and sweat is dripping into my eyes and down my cheeks. I can smell the sour stink of fear coming from my body. I try to call out to my father but all I can do is cough. The sharp smell of the smoke burns my nose and throat. My chest tightens as I cough again and again.

Then the door bangs open. "Nora!" calls my father, his voice muffled behind a towel. I stand and run into his arms. He throws me over his shoulder and runs out of the room. Smoke stings my eyes as we pass through the hall. He runs through the blazing *living room as I hang on, my face pressed into his back. The heat from the fire licks at my arms and the back of my neck. It's so hot that for a moment I think that I am on fire.*

We're out in the fresh air in moments. My father sets me down by a fence across the street. It's dark; the only light comes from our blazing apartment building. There are people all around, talking and shouting, the words jumbled together so I can't understand anything they are saying.

My father turns to face the fire. I hold on to his arm, which is slippery with sweat. It slides from my grasp as he moves away, back toward the hungry flames. I want to ask him where Mama is, to plead with him to stay, not to leave me alone. But I can't. No sound or words come out of my mouth. Then I realize I'm holding something. In my hands lies my father's watch, crumbling into ash . . .

I sat up on my mat, my heart pounding. I had fallen asleep staring into the candle's flames. It had burned all the way down into a puddle of cooling wax. It was still nighttime.

My eyes adjusted to the darkness and I sat still for a moment, looking around. Mama hadn't come home again. What could've happened to her? What would keep her from coming home two nights in a row? Where could she have gone? I scratched at my legs and realized I had left one side of the kulambo open.

"Well, it wouldn't do me any good to fix it now," I whispered, but my voice sounded loud in the stillness of the grave house.

I couldn't go back to sleep. I tried to lie on the mat again, using a piece of cardboard as a fan to keep mosquitoes away. I listened for Mama's footsteps, but there was nothing. I moved my mat closer to the bars so I could watch the alley from beneath the edge of the sheet. The lane was empty, except for a dog sniffing around for stray bits of food. I looked up at the night sky and the large golden moon.

Traces of the dream, like flashes of memory, continued to fill my mind. My eyes strayed from the moon to the moonbeam that had found its way between the sheet and the roof of my grave house. This small bit of light touched the embossed cement that bore Papa's name, the day he was born and the day he died. My vision blurred suddenly and I squeezed my eyes shut. What did the dream mean? Was Papa trying to tell me something?

"What should I do, Papa?" There was no answer.

The tears continued to flow. If Papa hadn't died, I wouldn't be living in the cemetery, and Mama—well, she would be just Mama. I'd still be in school. I didn't miss the homework, but I missed being there with Evelyn.

I crawled to Mama's Santo Niño altar and placed a single everlasting daisy in front of it. "Please bring Mama home," I said in a voice barely above a whisper. Then I sat, hugging my knees to my chest.

Sometimes, I wished that Mama and I had died in the fire with Papa, and then we wouldn't have to be hungry or alone. There seemed to be nothing left to hope for. The watch and the money I had worked so hard to save were gone, and now—I didn't want to think about it anymore. I just wanted to sleep. Forever.

✳

I thought I was dreaming of the color orange, when I realized it was the morning sun shining though my closed eyes. My eyelids were crusty with sleep and my mouth had a sour taste to it. Ugh.

I scratched my mosquito bites, listening for sounds of Mama moving around on the other side of the tomb. Nothing. I was alone. My stomach twisted, my throat burned.

I smacked my hand down on the concrete floor. My palm stung and prickled. How could she leave me alone like this? It felt like my head would explode. I plucked the folded cardboard from its place above the hinges, pulled the gate open, and stepped outside in the clothes I had been wearing since yesterday. Small kids from neighboring grave houses were already out in the alley playing. It was late in the morning. The sun was already high in the sky.

Ernie ran to me waving his arms in the air. All he wore was a pair of blue shorts. "You're finally awake! Mang Rudy told me to tell you—Hey! Where're you going?"

I ran, Ernie's voice fading behind me. Mang Rudy's advice was the last thing I wanted to hear right now. What I wanted most was to find Mama. But where would I begin to look?

I had a vague notion of where she played mahjong, but I wasn't sure. She'd once mentioned a woman called Aling Mary and something about a funeral home. There were at least two on Bonifacio Ave. A low whine rose up my chest and out my throat. It was all I could do to fight the panic beating like bird wings in my chest.

I searched the faces of women I saw on the street, hoping that one of them was Mama.

There was a woman wearing the same color dress Mama had been wearing the last time I saw her.

I ran and grabbed her arm, but it wasn't Mama. The woman stared at me, and then pushed me away.

I kept walking and found that I had wandered off the main road. My heart hammered in my chest. A strange buzzing filled my ears. The edges of my vision blurred. Where was I? I ran up the street and looked at the tombs around me, trying to find something I recognized, but nothing looked familiar.

What was happening to me? The world around me seemed to spin faster and faster. A wave of nausea spread up from my stomach. I gagged and fell to my knees, my pounding heart echoing in my ears. The sudden sharp pain of bare skin scraping rough concrete helped to calm me a little. I squeezed my eyes shut. I tried to focus on my stinging cuts but the dizziness remained.

I could hear the rapid slapping of slippers against the heels of someone's feet. The sound was coming toward me.

The tears in my eyes blurred the stranger's face. All I could see was a person wearing a blue baseball cap.

Oh my God. He must be one of Tiger's friends. I had to get out of here. I struggled to my feet, my dizziness making me weave as I moved forward. The world continued to spin around me and the sound of my breathing grew harsher as I stumbled. My mind screamed over and over. *Get away. Get away. Get away.*

Someone grabbed my arm. I struggled to pull away, but then somehow my legs just couldn't go on, and they buckled. I fell. The concrete street rushed up to greet me, its tiny holes and pockmarks coming into sharp focus. Then a dark brown arm thumped hard against my cheek and caught me before I hit the ground.

"Nora, what's wrong with you?"

It was the last thing I heard before the world turned black.

Chapter Nine

My body felt like a sack of rice, heavy and hard to move. I couldn't remember the reason why at first and concentrated on simply breathing in and out. In and out. A breeze lifted a strand of hair off my cheek. Paper rustled. Someone stirred a pot of something that smelled like—chocolate.

"Is she awake?"

"Don't talk so loud, Lola. You'll . . ."

"Poor thing! How could her mother . . ."

"Shhh!"

"How dare you shush me! Don't forget who you're talking to."

"Sorry, Lola."

Mama. My chest felt like it would burst. Everything that had happened in the last two days came back in a rush. Mama's disappearance. Tiger's unexpected, unwanted visit. Papa's watch, stolen. My lip trembled. I wasn't going to cry. Where was I? My eyelids opened a crack. In front of me sat Jojo in a faded basketball jersey, his face only inches from mine.

"Aha! You finally opened your eyes. Hey, Lola! Nora's awake." He handed me a glass of something warm as I pushed myself up on one elbow. "What happened to you out there?"

I shook my head. I remembered Jojo holding me up and carrying me on his back to his shanty, then nothing. I turned away. My face felt swollen from all the crying.

"Anak, go on, eat. You look like you need it. And you, stop asking her questions until she gets something in her stomach." It sounded like Jojo's grandmother whacked him on the head with her fan.

"Lola!" Jojo rubbed the top of his head, even though it probably didn't hurt, considering the fan was made of woven palm leaves.

The warm glass shook in my trembling hands. The spoon inside rattled against the glass. It had been a long time since someone was this kind to me. How could they be nice to someone who wasn't related to them? Lola Fely was family, and look where that had gotten me. I gripped the glass a little harder so that I wouldn't spill. Inside was a thick rice porridge, chocolaty and sweet. My mouth watered. I ate a spoonful. Then I ate some more. The chocolate and rice porridge warmed my stomach and eased the knots of pain I had been feeling since Mama disappeared.

Disappeared. No, I wasn't going to say that. Not yet. I mean, she could be anywhere, hurt probably, or sick or something. Something.

Lola Mercy was a small woman who walked slightly bent at the shoulders. Her white hair was pinned into a tight bun at the nape of her neck. Sometimes, strands of it escaped and framed her small face. She had a large brown mole right between her eyebrows that she claimed was the reason for her long life. It was the first time I'd seen the inside of Jojo's shanty. I'd only been as far as the front door to deliver their washed clothes or some gift of food from Mama. Lola Mercy would always invite me in but I was too shy to accept. It was a single room built from bits of wood and corrugated metal. Pinpoints of light filtered through gaps in the roof and walls like tiny stars. The curtain that covered the window next to me billowed gently in the breeze.

I was finished with the porridge, the glass practically clean again after I used my spoon to scoop out bits that clung to the sides.

"Thank you for the champorado, Lola." I wasn't sure if she actually cooked the porridge since she didn't have anything to cook on, but I thought it was more polite to assume that she did.

"My next-door neighbor has a little stove and she lets

me cook there a couple of times a week. Of course, I always give her a share of what I make as a thank-you. Honestly, I think her kids are grateful that I do. I've tasted her cooking. Terrible!" She made a face, and then smiled again, amused by her own criticism.

She shuffled over with a grin that not only showed off her toothless gums but wreathed her face in a starburst of wrinkles. Her eyes twinkled between the folds of her eyelids.

"Do you want some more? I made a whole pot full, so you can have as much as you like." Then in an exaggerated whisper, she pointed to Jojo and said, "Don't worry about him. He's too fat. He doesn't need to eat."

I giggled in spite of myself because Jojo was as slim and straight as a bamboo pole.

"Hey!" Jojo complained through a mouthful of porridge. He sat on the floor next to the bed I was sitting on. The bed was surprisingly soft. The cot sank a little when I pressed my hand on it.

"Nice, huh? I found a bunch of foam lying on a street corner. You know, the kind they use for cushions? So there was this stack of foam in different sizes. I guess they were scraps, but they looked useful to me. Can you believe someone actually threw this away?" Jojo lifted up the thin blanket to show me pieces of green foam piled on top of wooden crates. "My grandmother has one just like it over there."

Sure enough, next to the other wall stood another set of

crates with a homemade foam mattress on top. In the corner next to it was a chamber pot, in case his grandmother had to urinate in the middle of the night.

Lola Mercy came and sat next to me. She shooed Jojo away with her fan. She smelled like menthol, and I noticed small patches of what looked like white tape on her neck and upper back. Ah, so that was what I smelled. Salompas. A painkiller you absorbed through your skin. Mama used to cut small pieces off the medicinal patches and stick them to her temples whenever she had a headache.

"So what happened, anak?"

I didn't know where to begin or if I even wanted to talk about it. My eyes burned with the effort to hold back my tears, but one look at Lola Mercy's face, so kind and filled with concern, broke the shell I had so carefully built around myself.

She pulled me to her and rubbed my back as I cried. My world felt empty, hollow. I was alone. I didn't want to think about the things that might have happened to my mother. I just needed to find her.

After an hour (though it felt much longer) I felt a little calmer. It was time to go and start my search. My stomach no longer felt empty and I could stand without my legs wobbling. The champorado was exactly what I had needed. Warm gratitude filled my chest.

"Salamat po, Lola. I'll go home now. I don't want to give you any more trouble." Or run the risk of wearing out my welcome. Again. The memory of Lola Fely's sour face was still clear in my mind. I needed my mother, my family, and no one else. It strengthened my resolve to go and look for Mama.

"What? Leaving already? You have to rest!"

"I'm okay, really I am. I have to go home. Mama will worry if she gets there and I'm not there waiting for her." I had a feeling she would keep me here if I told her I was going on a search for my mother.

Lola Mercy and Jojo exchanged a knowing look.

"What is it?"

Jojo wouldn't look at me. He sat there, his mouth pursed as if to whistle, his eyes on the floor. Lola Mercy grunted and nudged him with her foot.

"Haven't you told her?" She nudged him again, this time a little harder.

"Aray!" He jumped up off the floor and rubbed his thigh with a mock expression of pain on his face. "It's just a rumor!"

"What are you talking about?" What was he keeping from me? My heart hammered in my chest so hard I couldn't breathe. Jojo looked at his grandmother sheepishly, then turned to me.

"I didn't want to tell you about it until I knew more and could check it out for myself," said Jojo. His grandmother turned away and carried the dirty dishes to a basin full of water under a window. Jojo watched her for a moment, and then looked at me, his eyes pleading with me to not be angry with him.

"Just tell me." It was hard to sit still. I wanted to shake the words out of him.

"I was talking with my buddy at the water pump this morning and asked him what he knew about Tiger."

I wanted to say that I didn't listen to gossip, but I kept my mouth shut. Maybe there was a chance I'd learn something, anything about what had happened to Mama. So many possibilities were running through my mind. I wanted to hear what the rumor was, and at the same time, I didn't. How bad could it be? Then I realized that it could be really bad.

"He said that he saw your mother get into a taxi with Tiger outside the cemetery gates the other day. He said that your mother owed Tiger's boss a lot of money, that she was in big trouble. He—he thinks Tiger killed her."

"What?!" My voice came out like a scream. I clamped my hands over my ears, shaking my head as if I could jerk the words out of my brain. "Noooo! Please don't say she's dead! She's coming back. I know she is."

I couldn't breathe. My chest tightened with each gasp. Lola Mercy rushed over and rubbed my back. Her warm hands eased my rising panic.

"That's enough, Jo. That was just a rumor. You're right, Nora. I'm sure your mother will turn up." Lola Mercy shot Jojo a meaningful look. "I'm sorry we brought up such gossip."

Lola Mercy let go of me and came back with something wrapped in banana leaves. She held it out to me, along with a plastic bag. "Here you go. It's just a little cold rice and fried fish. Take it. Please. I can't have any extra food lying around or else Jojo will get too fat," she said with a wink. Then she patted my arm. "Try not to worry. I know it's hard to do, but if you don't, you will go crazy. Now, we have to talk about where you will be staying until your mother comes back."

"But . . ." A lump formed in my throat.

"Ah, ah, ah. It's decided. You will stay here with me. You can sleep on Jojo's bed. He will sleep at your grave house. I would offer to stay at your place, but my dear grandson has spoiled me. These old bones will not like cement floors." She tugged on Jojo's ear, and he grinned at her.

"But what if my mother returns?"

Lola Mercy looked at me for a moment and said, "Don't worry. You can go there during the day and if she comes home during the night, then I'm sure Jojo will come and get you, okay? Now, there is another question I need to ask you. Is there someone you can call or write to, in case— well, in case your mother doesn't return?"

The gentle pity in her eyes made me start to cry again. "No! I won't think about that. She will come back. She has to."

"Yes, of course, anak. It's just good to know there is someone you can contact just in case. Now think!" She raised her sparse eyebrows, making her forehead crinkle into little hills and valleys.

The first person that came to mind was Lola Fely. But

she would be the last person I would call. "I have an uncle in Davao. When we first moved to the cemetery, he was supposed to send us money so we could come live with him. We were supposed to call him to see when he could send us the cash. We used to buy the cheapest prepaid phone cards to stay in touch with Tito Danny. But Mama sold her cell phone a few months after we arrived."

So she'd have money for gambling, I wanted to say, but didn't. Maybe if Mama had kept her phone, we would be in Davao by now. "After that, Mama wrote to her brother a couple of times. For a few weeks, we would go to Lola Fely's home and ask the maid if there was a letter for us. But there was never a reply. The last time we were there, Lola Fely herself chased us away with a broom. Mama gave up writing the letters since there was no way to receive mail in the cemetery." I sighed. "I know Mama has his number written down in a notebook she keeps."

"Well, make sure you find it. Jojo and I don't have a cell phone. Do any of your neighbors have one you can borrow?"

Mang Rudy had one. Mama had the same kind, where you had to open it like a clam. Normally, I'd be too embarrassed to ask to use his phone, but if something happened to Mama, then I wouldn't have a choice. I nodded.

"Good." Lola Mercy gave my arm another consoling pat.

With the package of food safely inside the plastic bag, I thanked them both again and left. I thought about what Lola Mercy had said while I climbed down steep wooden steps to the ground below. Jojo's home was one of a whole

plant, whose leaves had begun to turn brown at the edges. Even our mats were tucked away, rolled up into tight cylinders. I changed into a pair of capris and a shirt, and tucked the balisong into the secret pocket inside my waistband. I was glad Mama had insisted on sewing these hidden compartments into all my clothes. Then I packed a few things to take with me to Lola Mercy's place later on.

"So," said Jojo, as he rubbed his hands together. "Where shall we go looking first?" He was making it sound like we were going on an adventure.

"I'm not sure." I thought back on some of the things Mama had said in the last few months about her gambling. This was going to be more difficult than I thought. I'd always tuned her out when she talked about the when, who, and what of her daily mahjong games. This was annoying. What a rotten time to be forgetful. I should've paid more attention to what Mama talked about.

Jojo stood with his hands on his hips, his face expectant. "You don't know, do you?"

I ignored him and wished he would keep quiet while I tried to think. My eyes bored into his, hoping he'd take the hint. Then I shifted my stare to his ear and past it to a calendar Mama had hung on the wall. It said *Mercado* in big red letters on top.

Mama had brought the calendar home only last week. She had said something about how nice "Rosie" was, and that she was a good mahjong partner. From what I could recall, Mama had begun playing at Mercado Funeral Home after she met this woman. There had been a string of all-night vigils at this place for the past three weeks. The visitors played cards or mahjong in order to stay awake. I always thought it was just an excuse to gamble. As if a dead person would care that someone stayed up all night to watch over them.

Jojo quirked an eyebrow up and asked, "Well?"

"Let's start with Mercado's," I said, and headed out the door. I looked at Jojo's clothes. He was in a tank top and shorts as usual. "Don't you think you should at least put on a T-shirt?"

He looked down at his clothes. "Nah, no one will care. Besides, I like to save my T-shirts for special occasions."

I rolled my eyes and said, "Oh, all right. Let's go before I lose my nerve."

I asked Ernie to watch my grave house, since I couldn't lock it. Then Jojo and I headed for the cemetery gates.

The funeral home was a gray cement building with wide-open double doors in front. There were other kids around our age milling in and out of the entrance. I glanced down at my shirt and capris. It was a good thing I had changed my clothes. I hoped no one would pay too much attention to Jojo and me.

The front room was large, and in it was an open coffin laid out on an ornate platform between two blazing electrical lamps. Pews had been set up in front of the casket for visitors. Groups of people were sitting there, praying the Rosary. Others were gathered around a table loaded with sandwiches, stir-fried noodles, and eggrolls.

I ignored the saliva pooling in my mouth and followed a clacking noise that sounded like someone shaking a bag of marbles. The door opened onto a patio that held two tables and chairs, and a long wooden bench against the wall. One of them was empty, but at the other sat four women mixing a pile of mahjong tiles. There was a guy in jeans and a T-shirt standing nearby, watching the women play.

The mahjong tiles were jade green on one side and creamy white on the other. Pictures of flowers, balls, or Chinese characters flashed in and out of view as the pieces were mixed. I watched as a woman made rows of tiles stacked in neat green lines.

"Come on," whispered Jojo. He tugged me away from the door and pulled me toward the coffin. "We should at least look like visitors and pay our respects."

"Hey, but we don't know this guy." My hand flew to my mouth. There were people around us, but luckily no one was paying attention. Jojo dropped my wrist and right in front of me was the peaceful face of a dead man.

He was old, dressed in a Barong Tagalog of fine ivory cloth. The gauzy pineapple-leaf fabric was covered with elaborate embroidery in the same color. His hair was as white as the satin pillow his head rested on. He looked like he was sleeping. Papa had looked the same way, his brow smooth, and the crease that had always been there was gone.

Unlike this old man, Papa's hair had been black and thick, combed in a different way to hide the ugly gash made when the roof collapsed on him. He had also been dressed in a Barong, but a much simpler one. The memory made my eyes blur. I blinked and tears dripped down to my chin and dropped onto the glass that covered the opening of the coffin.

There was no time to think about Papa now. I had to concentrate on finding Mama. I wiped my face and stole a quick glance outside. It looked like the women were finished playing mahjong. I had to be fast if I wanted to ask them if they knew anything about my mother.

"Jo, let's go talk to those people outside before someone figures out we're not supposed to be here." A hand rested on my shoulder just then, and I knew we were caught. Would they make us leave before I had the chance to find anything out?

"Oh, you must be my husband's students! Your classmates were here earlier and said that a few of you would be late." A woman with short silver hair smiled at us and offered me a tissue from the pocket of her black dress. "It's a blessing for me to see how well-loved he was by his students."

"Oh, we're not . . ." But before I could finish my sentence, Jojo pulled me behind him and murmured something about condolences while I wiped my eyes in confusion. Then to my surprise, the widow led us to the food table, encouraging us to eat as much as we wanted.

Jojo wasted no time. He heaped noodles and eggrolls onto a plate and shoved it into my hands. I walked out onto the patio, hoping the mahjong players hadn't left yet. To my relief, three of the women were still sitting at the table. The guy I'd seen earlier was now playing.

Jojo followed, handing me a bottle of orange soda. Royal True Orange, my favorite. The sweat on the bottle sparkled like diamonds. I couldn't remember the last time I had had one.

The empty table was set for cards or mahjong, not for eaters, but we sat there anyway. Mahjong tiles were stacked neatly in piles in the center. The players at the next table paid us no attention at first.

Then one of them glanced up from her tiles and said, "Hoy! Alis! That table is for mahjong players. Go sit over there."

She pointed to a bench where a few people were already sitting, chatting and eating. There was room on the bench, but none of them moved over. They ignored us and acted as if we weren't there. Jojo shrugged, and signaled me to follow him to the planter next to the mahjong table. We set our drinks there and sat cross-legged on the patio floor.

The smell of the food filled my senses with a need so powerful, I soon forgot about the mahjong players and the snobs sitting on the bench. Concentrating my attention on the people next to me was completely smothered by my need to eat. I squeezed slices of calamansi over my noodles and shoved a forkful into my mouth. The rich flavor of pork and soy sauce, and the tartness of calamansi juice, exploded on my tongue.

It reminded me of birthdays at home. Mama would

make pancit canton, a pan-fried noodle dish with tender pieces of meat and crunchy vegetables. She'd let me invite my friends over after school to have some. The next mouthful was in my mouth almost as soon as I swallowed the first one.

When I had scraped the last of the noodles off my plate, I found Jojo staring at me while he slowly chewed his food.

Blood rushed to my face just then and made me look away shamefully. I must've looked like a dog eating the leftover scraps from its master's plates. Mama had always warned me about eating too fast. She always said it was bad manners to eat like you were starving to death. That was before we lived in the cemetery, before the fire. She didn't say it anymore, but I still felt ashamed.

"That was good," I said, taking a sip of orange soda.

"Ya-ar, am-am," said Jojo through a mouthful of noodles. When he tried to swallow, he choked. He was fine after I smacked his back a few times.

"Thanks," he sputtered. He had a noodle stuck to his chin. "You hit pretty hard for a girl."

"It's a good thing I can or you would've choked to death."

Grinning, Jojo stuck his tongue out at me. Then he drained his bottle of orange soda in a few gulps. He wiped his mouth with the back of his hand and went inside to get more food.

I sipped my soda slowly, waiting for the right moment to interrupt the game and ask questions.

The mahjong players were silent except for the occasional "Pong!" One of them picked up a tile with a grin of satisfaction. He tilted his row of game pieces onto their backs to signal his win. The women clucked their tongues and handed over their bets.

Mama had learned the game of mahjong from Papa, who used to play with his cousins when we visited them on New Year's Day. A couple of years ago, when I was ten years old, there had been a bad typhoon. Our neighborhood streets were flooded. School was canceled. Even Papa had stayed home from work.

Rain hammered down on our thin roof, drowning out the sound of our small television, making it impossible to enjoy any of the shows. Later in the afternoon, the sky grew darker, the wind louder, whistling through gaps between the walls and windows of our home. When the electricity went out, Papa lit candles in our small kitchen and set a flat, rectangular box down on our table.

"What's that, Papa?"

"I'm going to teach your mother a game." He opened the latches and lifted the lid. Milky-white blocks etched with red, blue, and green pictures lay in neat rows. Each one had a different design. Some had Chinese characters, and others had bamboo sticks or circles with numbers on the corners, like playing cards.

"Mahjong! Can I play too, Papa? Please?"

He ruffled my hair. Then I felt my mother's hands on my shoulders.

"You can, but don't tell anyone. Other grown-ups consider

playing mahjong a bad habit, especially when played for money. We will only play for fun and when the weather is bad," said Mama.

I rested my head on her chest and looked up at her. She smoothed back my hair and then kissed my forehead.

Papa showed us how to form lines of tiles, facedown, stacked two rows high. Then we each chose a line of thirteen pieces. He explained we had to get a pong, kong, or chow, and what it meant. It was like getting three of a kind, four of a kind, and a straight in cards. Papa said if we had four of these plus a pair, we would win the game.

We played for an hour, and then we had dinner. Mama had wanted to play some more, but I didn't, and just watched them. I had fallen asleep to the sound of the tiles clicking together as Mama and Papa played into the night.

A voice pulled me out of my memory so fast, it felt like someone poured cold water over my head.

"Rosie just got through taking our money. Now you're doing it!" said a woman with short dark hair and silver-rimmed glasses.

Mama's friend. She was here! I almost dropped my soda bottle. My hands shook a little when I set the bottle down in front of me, trying to listen but pretending not to.

"It's too bad she couldn't stay," said a woman with a ponytail. "Too busy at home, I guess. Strange. And her friend hasn't been coming around either."

"That's Lorna you're talking about. I can't say I've missed her. She always brings too little money and ends up borrowing from me to keep playing," said the woman with glasses.

"Really? She owes me money too. Those two are like peanuts in a shell lately. Always whispering. We have to keep an eye on them. They might be trying to cheat us," said the third woman, and pushed her tiles to the center. "So why do you think she was in such a hurry this afternoon?"

"Who? Lorna?" asked the guy in jeans, pocketing his winnings.

"No, silly. I meant Rosie," said one of the women.

"She said something about waiting for a phone call from Lorna when she got up to leave." He scraped his chair back and stretched.

A low buzzing filled my ears and blocked all sound.

Lorna. Mama. Rosie is waiting for a call from Mama.

I stood up so fast I knocked my drink over. Orange soda bubbled onto the patio floor, but I didn't care. All I could think about was this woman, Rosie, and that she might know where Mama was.

"Sir?" The man ignored me. I tugged on his sleeve. "Sir, please! Tell me where I can find Rosie. I have to talk to her."

He looked at me like I was crazy. "And why should I tell you?"

"Because I'm Lorna's daughter and I want to know where she is."

Chapter Eleven

It was almost dark. The streetlights flickered on hesitantly, as if waking up from a long sleep. I felt the same way. Rosie had become my glimmer of hope. My body felt full of energy; my spirits had lifted.

We didn't leave the funeral home until Jojo finished his second round of food. It took about that much time to convince those mahjong players who I was, and how important it was for me to talk to Rosie. I didn't tell them the whole story. In fact, I didn't tell them anything at all because they never gave me a chance.

"Look, before we tell you where to find Rosie, I want you to know how much money your mother owes us, so you can remind her when you see her again." The other mahjong players looked on, allowing this woman with glasses to hu- miliate me. "She owes me, Puring, one hundred pesos; she owes Cora seventy-five pesos; she owes Norma over there three hundred pesos; and finally, she owes Charito two hundred and fifty pesos. Now repeat it, so I know you were listening to me. Repeat!"

I did. It took all I had to stand there and listen to what they had to say, just to find out where Rosie lived.

I couldn't even think about the amount of cash Mama owed without cringing. It made me wonder if, all this time, the 'winnings' she'd brought home were pesos she had bor- rowed. Maybe she intended to pay an existing debt, but had spent or gambled it away instead. Mama used to be- lieve in making her own money, not asking other people for it. What had made her so desperate? Was this what gambling did to a person? When I saw her again, I would tell her to stop all of it. I would remind her that I could help her, and together we could stay alive. *If I see her again.* Strangely enough, knowing about her debts didn't make me angry with Mama. It just made me feel sad.

"Which street did she say it was?" asked Jojo. We stood at a corner a few blocks down the street from the funeral home.

"This one."

The sign said *Santa Inez St.* The street was so narrow we had to press ourselves against the fences to let a car pass.

Some children were playing on the pavement and we asked if they knew Rosie. They nodded, pointing to a two- story pale green house with a red fence.

The gate was open. There was a woman standing just inside, talking to a skinny guy in a blue baseball cap with matching blue sneakers. The woman gestured wildly with her hands as she spoke. The man began yelling at her, pointing a finger within an inch of her face. She slapped his hand away. The guy grabbed her wrist, leaning close. Then he let her go and left.

There was something familiar about the guy. It was the malicious set of his mouth, the hooded eyes, the pale patches on his skin. He looked at me and smiled.

Him.

Tiger had the baseball cap pulled low over his face. He sauntered toward us. The very sight of him made my stomach churn. A tingle of fear electrified my whole body, making my hair stand on end. Papa's watch gleamed on his bony wrist. It made me want to knock the stupid hat off his head.

Jojo must've recognized him, because he grabbed my elbow and pulled me to his other side, placing himself between Tiger and me. There was a scowl on his face that would've made anyone under the age of fifteen run away in fear, but not Tiger. If anything, his smile got bigger as he looked from me to Jojo and back again.

"Hey, you hang out with the water boy? I guess losers make friends with other losers, eh?" Tiger sneered.

"Shut up!" Jojo made a sudden move as if to hit him, but I held him back. The last thing I wanted was for him to get hurt because of me.

"What are you going to do? Fight me? Don't you remember what happened to your stupid friend?" Tiger laughed. The sound of it made me want to grind my teeth.

"Hayop ka!" Jojo yelled more curses than I knew existed. They came out so fast he practically growled them at Tiger. My hands were locked around Jojo's arm, but they were slipping fast.

The woman at the gate was still there, watching us. Was that Rosie? What was she doing? Why didn't she come and help us? I waved to her and screamed, "Help!"

She didn't hear me. Her eyes were fixed on Tiger.

Jojo tried to attack Tiger again and again, shouting and kicking. I could tell he was crying without seeing his face. His voice broke a couple of times.

"No!"

I lost my grip on his arm. He shot forward, head-butting Tiger in the stomach, and pushed him against the fence.

"Somebody help us, please!"

The children playing nearby stopped and watched. One of them ran farther up the street and into one of the houses. I noticed that the woman at the red fence was gone, the gate was closed.

We were on our own.

Jojo had Tiger pinned to the wall, punching him in the stomach. I pulled at his shirt and screamed his name over and over while my mind screamed, *Stop.*

Tiger grabbed Jojo by the hair, kneed him in the face, and then pushed him into my arms. It sent us both tumbling into the street. Jojo covered his nose with his hands, blood dripping through his fingers.

A hiss escaped through Tiger's clenched teeth. His eyes and nose were pinched together in anger. He stood over Jojo, a wicked grin spreading on his face when he saw the blood oozing out of Jojo's nose. "You're gonna regret you ever tried to mess with me." Then he kicked Jojo in the stomach.

Jojo curled into a ball and Tiger began kicking him everywhere—his back, his head, and his legs. *Oh my God. He's going to kill him.* I had to stop this. But what could I do? I felt paralyzed, my feet rooted to the concrete. *Do something.* I could ram my body into him, the way Jojo had a moment ago. I forced myself to move. Tiger must've seen me coming because his hand whipped out and punched me in the chest. The blow knocked me backward. I didn't have time to break my fall and landed on my back, hard.

Something clattered on the concrete next to me.

The balisong lay half open on the ground. I'd kept it in the secret pocket of my capris since Jojo had given it to me. I'd forgotten I had it. I snatched it up, releasing the blade. The wooden pieces that covered it folded back into a handle. My hands shook, but I gripped the knife as hard as I could and faced Tiger. He was bending over Jojo, checking his pockets for money.

"Get away from him!"

I pushed Tiger as hard as I could. He turned and swung at me. I raised my arm to block his blow when I heard him hiss in pain.

He stepped back a little, cradling his forearm. He stared at me, his eyes mere slits, his mouth set in a grimace. Blood poured from a gash in his arm. A smear of blood glistened on the tip of the balisong. I could feel my cheeks twitching into a smile. I'd gotten him and I wasn't even trying. Courage surged through my veins like fire. I could do this.

What did Jojo call it? The balisong dance. The knife whistled through the air in a flash of silvery light. Tiger involuntarily took another step back, almost tripping over Jojo's sprawled legs. *He's afraid, he must be.* But his eyes didn't lose that menacing look.

"You think a little girl with a knife is gonna scare me?" He lunged at me and tried to grab the weapon out of my hands. I slashed the balisong through the air once more.

"Ay!" Tiger stumbled back. He grabbed his hand, blood pooling in his palm. I jabbed and waved the knife, screaming like I'd lost my mind. The sight of Jojo lying on the ground woke up something inside of me. I had to do something to help, or give in. And I wasn't about to do that.

Tiger backed away. He growled something I couldn't understand and then ambled down the street. I made sure he was completely out of sight before I dropped the knife.

Jojo struggled to sit up. "Is he gone?"

I knelt beside him, a sob escaping from my mouth when he turned his face toward me. His nose and mouth were swollen and a dark bruise had begun to form on his cheek.

"Yes," I whispered, my heart still pounding.

He nodded and fell back against the ground with a sigh.

Chapter Twelve

"NORA." IT SOUNDED LIKE HE HAD SAID *MORA*. JOJO looked at me through swollen eyes.

With a lopsided smile, he said, "You're pretty good with a knife."

I couldn't help smiling back.

I helped him stand, my arm wrapped around his waist. We turned to head for home. I wondered how long it would take us to walk back to the cemetery. It seemed like such a long way.

"You dropped something." The woman from the gate stepped in front of us and handed me the balisong, folded and closed. She was younger than Mama but she had lines of hardship around her eyes and mouth. Her black hair was tied back in a low ponytail behind her head. She had a round face, with a sprinkle of freckles across her cheeks and nose. "Come to the house. Let's clean up your friend."

We followed her through the red gate. On the other side was a tiled patio with white-painted wrought-iron chairs and a glass-covered table. She gestured for us to sit and held a finger to her lips. She pointed to a window behind us, partially obscured by potted plants. Low voices and sad music drifted over to us from a television inside. The glow of it was visible through the screened front door. The woman disappeared around the side of the house. She returned with a small basin of water, a towel, and a bottle of alcohol.

She poured some of the alcohol into the water. Jojo flinched but said nothing when she pressed the cloth to his lip and wiped away the blood and dirt on his face.

"Umm . . ." I opened my mouth and shut it again when I remembered that she wanted us to stay quiet. So I whispered, "Are you Rosie? I need to talk to you. I'm looking for my mother."

Her eyes widened. "Are you Lorna's daughter? Oh my goodness, I wanted to go find you, but your mother never told me what part of the cemetery you live in."

She knows something!

"Is Mama okay? Do you know where she is?"

"No, I don't know where she is; that was one of the reasons why I was looking for you."

"Rosie? Who are you talking to out there? Is that rude man back? Maybe we should call the police," said a man in a voice that was as dry and whispery as rustling palm leaves. Rosie stood and peered over the plants in the window.

"Hindi, po! It's not that man. It's just my friend's kids." She sat back down with us and whispered, "I'm afraid you'll have to leave soon. My granduncle is very nice but he's old and not very patient."

"You work here? I thought you lived here, you know, as the lady of the house."

"Whatever gave you that idea? I'm just here to take care of him and make sure the house stays in order." She rolled her eyes for emphasis.

She finished cleaning Jojo up and placed the basin underneath her chair. "Look, I don't have much time so I'll be brief. I've been worried about your mother. She was supposed to meet me here yesterday for a game of mahjong. And when she didn't show, I thought that something must be wrong."

So she didn't know where Mama was or what had happened to her. Disappointment hit me like a punch in the stomach. But why would she think something was wrong because Mama didn't show up for a mahjong game? She already seemed to know that Mama had been missing for a couple of days. And then we saw her talking to Tiger. What was his connection to Rosie and Mama?

"What were you and Tiger arguing about?" I didn't care if she thought I was rude. Rosie looked down and then at Jojo, who was touching his lip and wincing. She seemed taken aback by the question. There had to be a connection.

"Oh, you mean the guy wearing the baseball cap? He

was being rude, like my uncle said. I told him to go to hell."
She hesitated, as if she wanted to say more. Then she looked
down, pressed her lips together, and said, "I really don't know
him that much."

"Please, Rosie, I need your help. Mama has disappeared
and I have a feeling Tiger has something to do with it. If
you don't help me, then I'll have to confront him myself." It
wasn't something I had actually considered doing, but if
I had to, I would.

Rosie's eyes shifted between Jojo and me. Then she
sighed and said, "Tiger works for Ruel Santiago, the owner
of Santiago's Grocery, who also happens to run a money-
lending operation on the side, among other things. My
uncle has borrowed money from him over the years. Tiger
and his gang collect payments for Mr. Santiago."

"How did he meet my mother?" My voice came out
stronger than I intended. Rosie signaled me to keep my
voice down as she peeked over the plants to check on her
uncle. I'd have to be more careful if I wanted her to keep
talking.

"A month ago, your mother came over after visiting
someone. I think she said it was her aunt. She was in a
pretty rotten mood and started grumbling about money. I
told her about Mr. Santiago. She asked me to take her to
his office. That was where she met him."

Mama went to visit Lola Fely? She'd never mentioned it
to me. I wasn't surprised that she came away from the visit
in a bad mood. Whatever it was, it had made her desperate.

"Do you know how much she borrowed? Did they do something to her because she couldn't pay it back? If you know what happened to her, please tell me."

"Rosie? Nasaan ka?" Her uncle grunted and mumbled to himself. A chair creaked and a pair of slipper-covered feet shuffled toward the door.

Rosie peeked over the plants and said, "Look, I've got to go now. I told you the truth. I don't know where your mother is, which is why I wanted to talk to Tiger in the first place. But I do have my suspicions."

"Rosie?" The old man was at the screen door. He was small and bent, like a bamboo plant caught in the path of a typhoon wind.

"I have to get my uncle ready for bed soon." Rosie jumped up and continued, "There was another reason why I wanted to find you. Wait here, I'll be right back."

Rosie went back into the house. She murmured something to the old man, who nodded and went back to watching television. When she returned, she handed an envelope to me. "Here, this came for your mother the other day."

It was a letter for Mama with Rosie's Santa Inez street address. I gasped. *It was from Tito Danny!* My mind filled with questions. "How—?"

"I would like to talk to you some more, but you'll have to come back another time."

She ushered us to the gate and out. The lock slammed shut behind us. It was fully dark now and the street lamps were bright. We stood under one of them and tore open the letter.

Jojo leaned in. "What does it say?"

My eyes scanned the cramped handwriting. It was short, just a few lines. I swallowed and read aloud. "It says—Dear Lorna, I hope this letter reaches you at this new address. Please know that I have received your other letters and replied to them promptly. I don't know why you never received them. In those letters I told you that my last litter of piglets didn't survive and I have been struggling to raise a new brood. I want you to know that this time, my pigs are doing well and I hope to sell them soon. Once I do, I will write to you again with instructions on how to pick up the money I will send. Please be patient, my sister. Give my love to little Nora. Your brother, Danny."

Jojo looked at me, waiting for me to say something. I folded the letter and stuffed it into my pocket. What was there to say? Did my uncle know about Mama's debts? When did Mama last write to him, and why had she decided to use Rosie's address? What had happened with Tito Danny's other letters? All I had were questions, and only Mama could answer them.

"Come on, let's go home," said Jojo.

I nodded and followed him down the street. I was glad he didn't ask me about Tito Danny or the money he wanted to send. Even if he did ask, I couldn't have brought myself to talk about it. I think he knew that.

Children were still playing outside. Their mothers stood by the fences, talking among themselves. They stared a little as Jojo limped by. No doubt they'd heard all about the fight from their children.

"Do you think she's telling the truth about your mom and Mr. Santiago?" said Jojo, pressing a hand to his rib-cage. "Ow, man, my side hurts."

"Hey, maybe you should see a doctor."

He barked out a laugh and then rubbed his thumb, index, and middle fingers together. I got it. No money. Well, he didn't look *too* bad. The more he walked, the less he limped.

I sighed. "Yeah, I think she was telling the truth. I just wish we had more time to talk to her."

"We can come back again tomorrow. Remember, you're staying with my grandmother tonight." He tried to smile at me, but it came out lopsided because of his swollen lip.

Yes, I did want to talk to Rosie again. Things were becoming more confusing. Had Mama tried to borrow money from Lola Fely? How much did she owe? My mind reeled through my mental list of her debts, including how much Mr. Santiago might have loaned her. Had she run away out of fear? Or shame? The thought made my eyes sting. How could Mama do this? Her gambling had made her blind and careless.

The number of questions was growing and the answers were few. Somehow I knew they would come, but would they be answers I could live with?

Chapter Thirteen

I'M HOLDING ON TIGHT TO PAPA'S WATCH. HE RUNS *back into the house where Mama must still be. The fire breaks through the roof, orange tongues of flame licking the night sky. Someone screams behind me. Mama is standing among the bystanders, clutching at them and screaming, "My house! My house is burning! Please help us! My husband, somebody get my husband!"*

Mama makes a move to run into the burning apartment, but people hold her back and tell her to wait. Then my head whips back to the fire, my breath suddenly catching in my dry, throbbing throat. I scream, "Papa! Papa!" but no sound comes out of my mouth. I run toward the flames. A line of men are passing buckets of water to some men standing on top of the next building, who are trying desperately to put out the burning roof. There is shouting everywhere, and the sound of sirens in the distance.

Why is Papa going back into the house? Doesn't he know that Mama is already outside, away from the fire?

Suddenly, there is a loud tearing, a groaning metal sound, that makes the men passing the buckets begin to scatter. One of them grabs me and pulls me away and cries, "It's going to collapse!"

He carries me, while I kick and struggle to get away, and sets me down next to a canal. I want to tell him that Papa is in there, that I have to get him out. Then with a crash, the roof of my house caves in with an explosion of sparks that begins to ignite new flames in neighboring buildings.

People around me run to put out the new fires as I stand there waiting for Papa to come out, believing that he will, that he will just walk right out through the fire. I shuffle slowly toward the burning remains of my home, while someone screams my name behind me . . .

"Nora. Nora, wake up."

I sat up and nearly fell out of Jojo's bed. Lola Mercy's surprisingly strong hands held me in place. My face was wet and my eyelids were swollen. They felt covered in mosquito bites and I wondered if maybe they were. But I knew I must've been crying all night.

"You were dreaming about your mother, weren't you?" Lola Mercy clucked her tongue and busied herself with making her bed in the dimness of her shanty. "Would you like some pandesal? Jojo dropped it off just a few minutes ago. They're still nice and warm. I tell you, Ibarra's makes the best . . ."

Ibarra's Bakery. Oh no. "Lola? What day is it?"

"I believe it's Wednesday. Something the matter?"

"No—I mean, yes. I was supposed to go back to work yesterday. There were towels and aprons to wash. Oh, Aling Lydia is not going to forgive me this time."

"Oh, nonsense, she will understand. Come, have breakfast."

After a quick kiss on Lola Mercy's papery cheek, I grabbed a roll and ran out the door with one word echoing in my mind. *Please, please, please.*

The last thing I needed was to lose my only means to stay alive. I slowed my pace to catch my breath, and hoped— no, prayed—that I still had my job.

Crowds of people clogged the street leading out of the cemetery. It was still early in the morning but the sun was high and hot. I hurried along, taking bites from the roll, bracing myself for the scolding I would get from Aling Lydia for being late again. I ran across the street and tried not to look inside the bakery. I didn't want to give Perla another chance to make a nasty remark.

But I did anyway. She seemed to be watching for me, because as soon as I looked at her she was already staring at me, smirking. I noticed that the girl who usually worked behind the counter with Perla wasn't there this morning. Instead, a teenage boy stood beside her, handing a customer their change. Mama had once told me that Perla had an older brother but I had never seen him. Could this guy be him? He was tall, with dark hair that fell in soft waves across his forehead. He had the same eyes and fair skin as Perla. But unlike his sister, his face looked kinder. He smiled and chatted with the customer he was helping. Too bad his sister wasn't more like him.

When I walked in through the front gate of the house, I found the porch empty. Aling Lydia usually waited for Mama and me to arrive so she could give us instructions and count the number of pieces there were to wash.

I was about to knock on the front door when I heard running water coming from the backyard. I walked toward the sound and peered around the corner of the house. The woman I met a few days ago with the mole on her chin was busy hanging towels while she filled the large palanggana with water. I hid when she started to turn my way. No wonder Perla was smiling.

My vision blurred as the tears started to flow. I rubbed furiously at my eyes and headed for the gate. I was almost there when I heard the front door open.

"There you are! I've been wondering what happened to you and your mother. You were supposed to come back yesterday, remember? What excuse are you giving me this time, huh?" asked Aling Lydia. She stepped out of the house wearing a duster and tiny pink rollers in her hair. She wagged a manicured finger at me and said, "Now you know that I meant what I said. I want to have reliable people working for me."

"I'm sorry, po. Please, let me explain. My mother . . ."

"I know your mother has problems."

"That's what I'm trying to tell you. My . . ."

"No more excuses, Nora."

"Please, just listen to me!"

The back door of the bakery banged open behind me. I knew without looking that Perla and her brother had come out to see what was happening.

I wanted to kick something. I did.

My foot somehow made contact with a dried coconut husk that someone had left by the patio. It sailed through the air and nearly hit Aling Lydia, who had been standing with her hands on her hips. She didn't even flinch.

Perla's high-pitched voice suddenly filled the air, accusing me of trying to hurt her mother. She would have screamed more hurtful words if her brother hadn't stopped her by explaining that it was an accident.

Aling Lydia paid her children no attention. She stepped off the patio and stood directly in front of me.

"I'm sorry, Nora. But I had to give the job to someone else. You were supposed to show up yesterday. I was counting on you. You've become as unreliable as your mother. And now you show up making excuses."

"I'm not!" I didn't mean to shout, but I could feel my desperation and anger becoming a living thing inside me.

Aling Lydia paused, her eyes narrowing, and her mouth formed to say more poisonous words. It had to stop.

"My. Mother. Is. Missing!" I screamed, each word flung

into the air between sobs. Afterward, I began to shake, not caring anymore what anyone thought about my mother or me. "And stop talking about my mother as if she's a bad person! You know nothing about her and what she's suffered and lost since my father died. All she wants is a better life for me." I sniffed, pulling up the neckline of my shirt to wipe the tears off my face. "She left to play mahjong on Sunday and never came back. I didn't come to work because I've been looking for her. She must be hurt or something because she wouldn't leave me, not ever."

The fire inside me diminished as the words flowed from my mouth. Perla and her brother stared at me, their angry expressions melting into shock. I could see it in their faces. How dare I speak to *their* mother this way. I was breathing hard. New tears flowed, cooling my hot cheeks.

"I'm disappointed in you, Nora. You have always been a polite girl." Aling Lydia walked over to where I stood, her hands on her waist, her lips pressed into a frown. She leaned down so that her face was only inches from mine. "I hope you're telling the truth. And if you are, then I will forgive your rudeness—*this* time." She stood straight again and sighed, regarding me with crinkled brows. "Look, I am not a cruel woman. If you need a place to stay, I can work something out. And since you've done well covering for your mother in the past, I can give you a job in the bakery. I do need someone to help out with washing pans and sweeping the floor. The job is yours if you want it. It's only temporary until your mother comes home. What do you say?"

I wanted to tell her that I had to stay in my grave house in case Mama returned. I wanted to thank her for offering me a place to stay and for giving me work. I wanted to yell at her again for not listening to me in the first place. But the words clogged in my throat and wouldn't come out. Instead, I turned away and cried, out of shame and anger.

I ran through the gate and was in the street the next moment. Aling Lydia called my name, telling me to come back, but I kept on running, away from the bakery, from the cemetery, as if I could run away from life.

What was I supposed to do for money now? How were Mama and I going to buy food and candles? I should at least march back to Aling Lydia's and accept the job. But I continued to walk. Tears filled my eyes until everything looked like a blurry mess. I couldn't see where I was going and I didn't care. All I wanted to do at that moment was scream, *It's your fault, Mama!* But I didn't, afraid that I wouldn't be able to stop. If only Papa hadn't died, if only Mama wasn't so careless. If only there was a way to escape or disappear forever.

I finally stopped at a street corner, surrounded by unfamiliar buildings. I sat by a wall to figure out what to do next when I noticed a group of girls walking up the street.

There were about four of them, probably students on their way to school. They wore maroon pleated skirts and white blouses with wide sailor collars. Thin maroon ties with embroidered letters hung at their throats.

I watched them as they talked and gestured. They were probably complaining about exams or about a teacher.

Evelyn used to do that. We were opposites when it came to schoolwork. I worked hard to get onto honor roll, and some months I did, just barely. But Evelyn made it every time. Where I would have been happy to make it on the list, my best friend fought for the number-one spot.

I wished I could talk to her. I missed school, even though I wasn't a top student. I understood that having a high school diploma would give me a better chance to find a job when I grew up. If I didn't finish my education, I'd have to be a street vendor. I stared at the girls in uniforms and wondered if they knew how lucky they were.

One of them had long, straight hair. She wore a headband that kept most of it out of her face. She looked familiar. Her skin was fair and smooth. She had a small dark mark above the corner of her lips. Nausea wriggled in my stomach like a worm. My mouth went dry and my throat felt like I had just swallowed a santol seed.

I know her.

There was only one person I knew with a beauty mark like that. It was Evelyn. I almost didn't recognize her. She looked so grown-up wearing a headband instead of braids. After the fire and Papa's death, I'd never gone back to school. I'd never had a chance to tell her what had happened to me.

I wanted to run to her and ask her about what classes she had and how our friends were doing. I wanted to but I couldn't. My shorts were frayed at the edges, the colors of the fabric so faded they looked old and dirty. My slippers had a hole, my feet were callused. I couldn't let her see me like this.

She was a few feet away when I got up. Would she recognize me? Probably not.

I walked away, glancing back at her one last time.

Evelyn had been whispering something to her friend. Our eyes met and locked.

"Nora? Is that you?" Her eyes roamed over my clothes, her brow wrinkling.

I froze. Every nerve in my body screamed with shame. *Run away! Run away!* But I couldn't. Evelyn's eyes grew large, wondering, as she took in my messy ponytail, my T-shirt and shorts. Her lips formed a small O. Then her hand shot up to her mouth.

Her eyes held mine as she approached. She took my hands in hers and said, "What happened to you? Why didn't you come to school last year? My mom told me there was news about a big fire in Mandaluyong. I remember seeing the smoke. She said that a couple of people died but she didn't know who it was. So where did you and your parents move to? Oh, I'm so happy to see you!" Evelyn pressed my hands between hers, her eyes shiny with tears. Her lips curled into a small smile. Then she opened her arms, my hands still in hers, spreading them wide. "You're not in uniform. Aren't you in school?"

Her friends looked at one another, then stared at my clothes, full of curiosity.

"Evie, I—I—my father died in the fire," I stammered, struggling for something to say and blurting out the only truth that mattered. I wanted to tell her that I didn't go to school, that Mama and I had run away from Lola Fely's unkindness, that we lived in a cemetery. But I couldn't. At least not in front of her friends.

Evelyn's smile dissolved into open-mouthed shock. She took in my appearance again and seemed to understand all the things I couldn't tell her.

"Oh, Nora. I didn't know."

She pulled me into a hug. Her friends had stepped away from us, looking embarrassed.

The feel of her arms around me, the smell of her clean clothes and her shampooed hair, made my eyes sting with tears. I wanted to hold her and not let go.

"Evelyn, we only have fifteen minutes to get to school," said one of her friends, looking between Evelyn and me.

"I'm sorry, Evie. I don't want you to be late."

"It's okay, Nora." My friend turned to her companions and said, "Just another minute."

She rummaged in her school bag for a piece of paper and pencil. I noticed her gold stud earrings and the wristwatch she wore. It made me feel more uncomfortable. She pulled out a notebook, tore out a page, and scribbled on it. Then she dug into her skirt pocket and pulled out a ten-peso bill. She shoved both into my hands.

"Here is my phone number. Call me. My father works at the bank now. I'm sure he can do something for you and your mother."

I should have felt happy that she wanted to help. I should have felt relieved that I had a friend who still remembered me. But I only felt embarrassed by her pity.

"I'll keep your phone number but I can't take your money." It was probably her jeepney fare. I pushed the money back into her hand and turned away as her mouth opened in protest.

I ran. My throat ached. Tears flowed from my eyes, blinding me.

"Nora! Stop!" Evelyn and her friends ran after me.

I ducked into a dressmaker's shop. The bell above the entrance jingled and a blast of cool air hit me, chilling the sweat on my neck and back. The door closed just as Evelyn reached it.

The bolts of fabric next to me made the perfect hiding place. I lowered myself into a crouch just as an old woman stepped out from behind a yellow curtain. The bell jingled again.

I heard her shuffling feet and then her voice. "Can I help you?"

The door thudded shut. "Good morning, po. I'm looking for a girl. She ran into this shop a minute ago."

I could hear the old woman move closer. "Oh, I'm afraid I haven't seen her. If she came inside, then maybe she has gone out again."

Evelyn's steps faltered, hesitating. She mumbled, "I could've sworn—" Then she let out a sigh and said, "Okay, thanks."

The bell jingled once more.

My heart hammered in my chest as the old woman shuffled through the curtain at the back of the store. I slipped out the front door. Evelyn and her friends were gone.

I wandered around the rest of the day, back to the cemetery. Confused, my head pounding, I began to cry again when someone grabbed me by the shoulder. I pulled away and screamed.

"Naku, I didn't mean to scare you!" said Mang Rudy. "I was walking home when I saw you come out of that shop. Hey, are you okay?" He was carrying a wooden rectangular box with tools inside.

I shook my head, my chest still heaving. My voice, when it came out, sounded like a squeaky wheel.

"I got lost." My lip quivered, tears streaming down my cheeks.

Mang Rudy handed me his handkerchief. It had grease and sawdust on it, but I didn't care. I wiped my eyes and blew my nose.

"Well then, it's a good thing I found you. Hey, shouldn't you be at work with your mother?"

"Mama hasn't come home." I swallowed. "I got my washing days wrong and Aling Lydia gave our job to someone else." Embarrassment heated my face. I remembered that it was Mang Rudy and his wife who had helped Mama and me get the labandera job at Aling Lydia's. "She did ask me if I wanted to work in the bakery instead. But I was too upset to give her an answer."

Mang Rudy's brow creased. He placed a hand on my shoulder and looked me in the eyes. "Wait—did you say your mother didn't come home?"

"Yes, she didn't come home Sunday night, and now it's Wednesday, and—" I couldn't continue. My throat tightened, and a painful sob fought to punch through.

He shook his head, making *tsk-tsk* sounds. He sighed and said, "Jojo did mention that you were staying with Lola Mercy last night. Now I understand why." He sighed again. "All we can do is wait and see. Remember that Aling Nena and I are here to help. We will do what we can for you."

"Salamat po." I did feel grateful. I could ask to use his cell phone. I remembered the piece of paper in my pocket with Evelyn's phone number. But I knew I couldn't call her. It was nice of her to think her father would help squatters like Mama and me. No, if something happened to Mama, I'd have to call Tito Danny. "I'll go back to the grave house. I want to be there in case she comes home."

If she comes home.

"Hmmp. That's too bad about the washing job. Working in the bakery would be better for you. You can learn to make pandesal. A good skill to have. It's hard to find work these days, especially for people like us. Come, let's go home. You can talk to Aling Lydia tomorrow." He patted me one more time on the shoulder and started walking home.

I wished that work was the only thing I was looking for.

Chapter Fourteen

I STOOD OUTSIDE JOJO'S SHANTY, LISTENING TO LOLA Mercy humming to herself. It reminded me of how Mama used to hum while she folded laundry. The memory brought back my tears. I had lost my job, Mama, everything. My heart was still pounding from seeing Evelyn. I took a deep breath to calm myself and concentrated on Lola Mercy's quavering voice.

It was that time of day, just before night, where everything outside took on a bluish cast. There were spots of yellow light coming from open windows in neighboring shanties and grave houses. The taps and scrapes of metal spoons and forks on plastic plates mingled with the muted conversations of daily living. It made me remember my old neighborhood. It was as if I were standing outside my old house and not a shack in the middle of a cemetery. The sounds were ordinary, even happy, in contrast to the emptiness I felt. I had no father. And now, no mother. I had denied the possibility that Mama had run away, but with everything I'd learned so far, it seemed the most likely explanation. But why hadn't she taken me with her? Why had she left me behind?

"Nora?" Lola Mercy peeked through one of the wide gaps between the old planks that made up the door. She flicked off the hook that kept it closed and took a peek before she swung it wide open, fanning vigorously. The sudden gust of air cooled the last tears on my cheeks.

"Pasok, pasok. Hurry, I don't want any more mosquitoes getting in here," said Lola Mercy.

Once I was inside, Lola Mercy closed the door and repositioned a dark green mosquito coil balanced on top of a metal triangle. The outer end of the coil glowed bright orange at its tip. A tendril of smoke drifted up from it and tickled my nose. It smelled like charcoal and candles. It brought back memories of sitting in a tiny living room with Papa, watching the news. We'd used the same mosquito repellent. I squeezed my eyes shut. I should have felt angry at how unfair life had been for me. But I felt nothing. This day had used up all that I had left.

Lola Mercy seemed oblivious to my stillness. I stood, staring into space in the middle of the shack, as she doled out what looked like rice porridge from a small pot. The smell of ginger and chicken broth made my mouth water. I hadn't eaten anything the entire day, besides that morning's roll. Lola Mercy sprinkled green onions and toasted bits of garlic on top of the porridge from two small plastic bags.

"Here you go, anak. You must be starving," said Lola Mercy as she handed a bowl to me. I inhaled deeply and was surprised to see a small piece of chicken on top of the creamy white bed of porridge.

Lola Mercy pulled a couple of benches from under the window and gestured for me to sit down.

"Salamat po." It was all my parched throat could manage. The bench was so low that my legs were folded close to my chest when I sat down. I balanced the bowl on my knees and ate a spoonful. The warm porridge slowly eased the tightness of my throat.

We finished our meal under the glow of a single golden light bulb. The only sounds came from Lola Mercy's slurping and from the *tap, tap* of the spoon against the plastic bowl. Lola Mercy's soft, smiling face made me wonder just how happy she was. I'd never heard her or Jojo complain. I wondered how long they had lived here.

"That was delicious, Lola. Jojo told me you were a great cook." The rice had been simmered to creamy perfection. It made my stomach feel warm and less hollow. She must've gone next door to cook again. Lola Mercy nodded and smiled, her eyes disappearing in the webbed creases and wrinkles of her face.

The dishes were washed using buckets of water she kept outside by the door. That was where I had to wash up and brush my teeth. Luckily, Lola Mercy had a chamber pot so I didn't have to relieve myself outside as well. Not having a bathroom was one of the most uncomfortable things about living here in the cemetery. When I first moved here, I hadn't bathed for a week. Mama had explained that all we had to do was take a bath with our clothes on. It was a year since that first time, but I'd never gotten used to it.

Jojo's bed was soft, a nice change from lying on a concrete floor with only a woven mat and a flattened box to sleep on. But last night, the wooden crates beneath me had wobbled and creaked. Even though it was comfortable, the unfamiliar sounds had woken me every time I changed position.

Lola Mercy sat on her bed, her legs tucked underneath her as she pulled a rosary from a pouch she kept pinned to her duster. She crossed herself and began to murmur gently. My mind wandered, my heart heavy. What was I going to do? Especially if—no, I wouldn't give up on Mama yet. No one, not even Tiger, could stop me from getting to the truth. The thought of him made my chest tighten, squeezing the air out of my lungs. The memory of what he'd done to Jojo made me cringe. We would have to be more careful. I couldn't handle another confrontation with him. I wished more and more that Mama and I had moved to Davao.

Lola Mercy was putting away her rosary while humming a tune that sounded familiar to me. It was a song by Sharon Cuneta, about being in love until you grow old and your hair turns white. Mama's favorite. She used to sing it to Papa all the time.

It was strange to see someone like Lola Mercy, who didn't seem to mind being a squatter. I suddenly had to know why.

"Lola?"

"Hmmm?" She stretched out on her bed with a satisfied sigh. "My old bones have been spoiled by this bed. I'll never be able to sleep on the floor again. Thank God for my grandson. He takes good care of me. You know, he reminds me of his grandpa, always thoughtful, always helpful. And a great charmer," she said, and chuckled.

"Lola, may I ask you something? How did you and Jojo come to live here in the cemetery? Did something terrible happen to you?" *Like me,* I wanted to say. Some squatters had moved to Manila from the provinces looking for a better life and had ended up here. What would Lola Mercy's story be?

"Oh, yes. Something terrible happened. At least, it was terrible for my parents. You see, I moved here because I got married."

She laughed at the expression on my face and continued, "When I met my husband, I was twenty years old and working at a T-shirt shop not too far from here. He came into the store to buy a shirt for his father. He smiled at me and I thought he was very handsome. I helped him find what he wanted to buy and we haggled over the price for half an hour. I tried hard not to look at him, because I didn't want to give him the wrong impression. Well, not only did he buy the shirt, but he came back every day at the same time with a snack to share with me, and we became engaged a few months later. We had a simple wedding at City Hall and a party at my parents' house. Then he took me home to his grave house."

"When did he tell you that he lived in the cemetery?"

"He told me from the beginning that he and his family lived at the Manila North Cemetery. I didn't believe him at first, so when he brought me home to meet his parents, I was shocked. Their grave house was a little bigger than the one you live in. His father was a stonemason, a caretaker of a family mausoleum. My husband was born in the cemetery, along with his three brothers. After we were married, we moved into the neighboring grave house. For the next thirty-five years, we lived there and had two children, Leticia and Roberto. Leticia was Jojo's mother. She married a cemetery boy despite our disapproval. We wanted so much more for her." Lola Mercy was quiet for a while, lost in a stream of memories.

"Lola, you said 'was.' What happened to Jojo's mother?" Jojo never talked about his parents. Whenever the subject came up, he would make a face and say that he didn't remember anything about them.

"Leticia married a young man who was always mixed

up in some money-making scheme. Most of the time, nothing ever came of it, and their life was hard. She washed clothes and whenever her husband could, he did carpentry work. He built this very place with whatever he could find. They seemed happy enough. When Leticia got pregnant, her husband worried about raising a child, but the excitement of having a baby erased all that. Leticia had a hard pregnancy and an even harder delivery. She didn't survive. She died here, with a midwife arriving too late to help her."

Lola Mercy's voice was down to a whisper. It quavered, and then stopped. With /a deep breath, she went on. "Leticia's husband handed me the screaming baby and said he would be right back. I thought he was going out to make arrangements for Leticia. We waited but he never returned. I stayed here for days, hoping Jojo's father would come back. The days turned into weeks, and I realized that this was where I would stay to raise Jojo, because this was where he was born and where my daughter died."

"What about your husband? What happened to him?" I could barely squeeze the words out. My throat throbbed with unshed tears. How did Lola Mercy keep going after such heartache? And what did Jojo think about it?

"Oh, my dear husband was devastated. It was the final blow to his weak heart. Before Jojo was born, my son Roberto went to seek his fortune in the southern islands. He wanted to dive for coral and rare tropical fish and sell them to foreign buyers. Naive boy! We tried to stop him. It was too risky. He left anyway. We had been waiting for months for news, for a letter, but nothing ever came. He never returned. Then after that, Leticia died. My husband passed away not too long after my daughter. They are both buried in the grave house I used to live in, where his brother now resides, and I am here with Jojo."

She sighed deeply. "And we have lived quietly, not asking for too much, always grateful for the little we have and for each other. I make some money selling roasted corn in the afternoons, and as you know, Jojo does all kinds of odd jobs, so we get by okay. My grandson is very smart, you know. And he's a hard worker. I just wish I had been able to put him through school." Lola Mercy's jaw cracked as she yawned. She murmured, "Hmm, it's getting late, my dear. You've had a long day. Get some rest." She closed her eyes and sighed. "See you in the morning."

"Goodnight, Lola." For the first time in a year, I began to understand why Lola Mercy and Jojo seemed so easygoing, so at ease with the way they lived.

I saw it in the way they took care of each other. Like those beds Jojo had made from foam so his grandmother wouldn't have to sleep on the floor anymore. How he pretended to be grumpy when his grandmother teased him about being too fat, and how her face crinkled into a smile when they were together. These memories made me feel warm, comforted.

That's what it is. Consuelo. Comfort. I know what this is now.

This feeling had surrounded me since Mama disappeared, even though I was too distracted, too confused, in too much pain to acknowledge it. But now it wrapped around me like a cocoon, sheltering me. Lola Mercy and Jojo had become more than friends. They were beginning to feel like family.

Jojo and his grandmother believed that if they helped one another and their neighbors, they would have suwerte, luck for the future.

Mama and I had been like them once. We'd wait for Tito Danny to call, or we believed that Mama's luck would change and she'd win enough money to get us out of the cemetery and home to Davao. Neither happened. Then our need to escape grew stronger, the longer we lived in the cemetery. I hadn't just wanted to stay alive; I knew that I wanted my old life back, and I wanted Mama to be her old self before the gambling. But maybe we could think of a better plan to leave the cemetery and be more hopeful too.

I balled my hand into a fist. *We still have a plan.* Like Jojo and his grandmother, all we needed was patience. We would pay back the money Mama owed. I could keep up my studies with Kuya Efren. I could call Tito Danny somehow. I could take the bakery job Aling Lydia offered. We had friends who encouraged us. I had to believe that as long as I had Mama with me, we would have a better life someday in Davao.

But first, I have to find you, Mama.

Chapter Fifteen

THERE WAS A LOUD *BANG*. MY ARMS JERKED AND THE sheet I was folding fell out of my hands. Lola Mercy had dropped the kettle and was bent over attempting to retrieve it as it rolled in circles on the floor.

When she straightened up, she was frowning. "You shouldn't go back there. It's not safe."

Lola Mercy was usually the calmest person I knew. Even when Jojo had come home the other night with his face bruised and swollen, she calmly cleaned him up. When we told her what had happened that night, she listened without comment. But there was nothing calm about her this morning.

She had been rinsing her old kettle and telling me about

her neighbor, the one who couldn't cook, who made coffee in a pot so large, a small child could fit inside. The coffee was sold by the pot or cupful, and Lola Mercy had conceded that it was the best she had ever tasted. She had asked me what I was planning to do today. I had told her I wanted to talk to Rosie again.

"What are you thinking? If Tiger shows up at that woman's house again, what are you going to do?"

"But Lola, Rosie might know something important. She told me to come back so I could ask her more questions."

"No. Absolutely not." Lola Mercy waved the kettle in the air for emphasis. "And that goes for my grandson too, wherever he is."

"Breakfast time!" Jojo popped in through the door. He startled his grandmother so bad she dropped the kettle again. He picked it up for her and earned a scowl for his attempted apology. Lola Mercy shuffled out the door to buy her coffee, muttering to herself the whole time about crazy kids and how she was too old to deal with them.

"What's wrong with her? I thought she'd be happy to have suman for breakfast," said Jojo after handing me a bundle of hotdog-shaped sticky rice cakes, each one wrapped in yellow-green buli leaves and tied together with a strip of palm leaf.

"I told her we were going to Rosie's today."

Jojo looked thoughtful, then shook his head in understanding while he took a plate from the shelf.

What were we going to do now? I didn't want to upset

Lola Mercy, but at the same time, I needed answers from Rosie.

There was nothing to do but wait for Lola Mercy to return. Nervousness bounced around in my stomach like a firefly trapped in a bottle. Would she still be upset when she came back? It was hard to tell from the singsong rhythm of her voice as she chatted with the woman next door.

The flutter in my stomach turned to grumbling when I untied the strip that held the bundle together and placed the wrapped cakes on the plate. They were still warm; the sweet, green, nutty smell of palm leaf and coconut milk filled my nose. It made me hungry and homesick at the same time. When I was little, Mama used to make suman and sell it to our neighbors and to my teachers at school. Sometimes she couldn't sell all of them, and so she served them every day for breakfast until Papa and I complained. The sight of them used to make me so nauseous that I avoided them whenever possible. But not today. I wanted to eat them so I could keep that small memory of Mama's suman vivid in my mind and heart.

Most of the sticky rice cakes were unwrapped by the time Lola Mercy came back with her kettle full of coffee. She was humming. I took it as a good sign. I was wrong.

"Hmmp. Needs sugar," said Lola Mercy after scrutinizing the rice cakes on the plate. She set the kettle down on the floor, passing out three glasses for coffee and a small covered jar of sugar.

Lola Mercy tucked her duster between her legs and folded her body into a squat. She poured the coffee and opened the jar of sugar. She dipped a suman into the jar. "Nora told me you two plan on visiting that woman, Rosie. Is that right?" She held up her hand when she saw my mouth open to answer her. "Let him answer, Nora."

"Uh-huh. But not until this afternoon. I have to do my water run, and Nora wanted to go home so she can, you know, wait for her mother. Just in case." He didn't seem disturbed by the look his grandmother gave him. He just picked up a suman, peeled away the palm leaf, and dipped the rice cake into the jar. He bit into it, spilling sugar down his chin.

"Well, I don't like it. Look at what Tiger did to you, boy. You don't want to end up like your friend Teddy." Lola Mercy shook a rice cake at him, paying no attention to the sugar that spilled onto the floor.

I sat up a little straighter. My skin tingled. How could I have been so blind? This was the reason why Jojo had been so angry at Tiger the other night. Of course Lola Mercy would be upset. Jojo's best friend had been attacked and killed by Tiger's gang a year ago. Jojo had said that Lola Mercy was sure that if he were with Teddy that day, she would've lost him as well. Who was I to ask her to put Jojo at risk? He was her entire world.

I cleared my throat. "I'll go by myself."

Jojo and Lola Mercy looked at me, their mouths frozen in midchew. So I went on, hoping they'd take me seriously.

"I'll go while it's still light, when there are more people in the streets."

This time they stared at me open-mouthed. It was either because I had said something amazing or really stupid. Then they looked at one another. Lola Mercy sighed.

"Well, I can't let you go alone. If you insist that this woman has something to tell you about your mother, then you must go and ask her."

She gave Jojo a stern look, then turned to me with softer eyes. "Just be careful, anak. And make sure my knuckle-head of a grandson doesn't lose his temper again."

"Aray!" cried Jojo when his grandmother twisted his ear and pulled him into her arms. She gave him a noisy kiss on his cheek before he could pull away. Lola Mercy turned to me and asked, "Have you found your uncle's phone number? Have you tried calling him?"

"Not yet," I answered. "I'll give my mother one more day, then I'll call him tomorrow."

She squeezed my hand and patted it gently. Her hard-won approval was a relief. Jojo and I would be careful. Besides, we had our own small means of protection.

My hand pressed against the pocket of my shorts, making sure the balisong was still there. I was ready to face Rosie and all she had to tell me about Mama. Tiger or no Tiger.

✳

Bonifacio Avenue rippled with movement. People carried umbrellas or wore hats against the blazing sun. Light reflected off of bus windows and the chrome sidings of jeepneys crawling through traffic in both directions. Commuters on motorcycles wove between the cars, beeping their horns, warning drivers and pedestrians to look out. The humid air thickened with the smell of exhaust and sweat. I pulled up the neckline of my shirt to cover my nose. I didn't want to breathe in the soot that puffed out of exhaust pipes. It made your snot turn black.

Jojo and I nudged and pushed our way out of the main gate of the cemetery and walked to the corner of Bonifacio and Merced. I was rehearsing what I would say to Rosie in my head when a flash of silver and blue caught my eye.

The traffic was at a standstill. Cars and jeepneys honked their horns impatiently. On the far side of the street was a taxi with its windows rolled down. A hand dangled out with a cigarette clamped between its fingers. It wasn't the hand itself that caught my attention. It was the watch on the wrist. Papa's watch. Its blue face winked at me in the morning sun. I didn't have to look inside the car to see who the hand belonged to.

Inside the taxi, Tiger's head turned left and right, as if he was looking for someone. He even looked in my direction, but he didn't see me. Thank goodness for the crowd. The taxi jerked forward as the traffic eased up. There was someone else in the car beside him. It was a woman, leaning back with her head lolling to one side. The shape of her face looked familiar—my heart jumped.

Could it be Mama?

I watched the taxi as it turned into the cemetery gate. If that was Mama in there, and I hoped to God it was, then I had to stay with the car and never lose sight of it. It was the only way to be sure.

"Hey, what are you staring at?" Jojo bumped me as the crowd of people pushed us back toward the cemetery gate. Then a tall man stepped in front of me. His wide back blocked the taxi from view. I tried to jump and move around him. "What is it, Nora?"

"I saw Tiger in that taxi over there. There's a woman with him. I've got to get a closer look."

"I see it!"

We dodged through the crowd, heading back to the cemetery. The taxi paused at the gate.

Tiger was leaning forward, talking to the driver. The woman's face was visible now; her body sagged against the car door in an awkward way. "It's my mother! Come on. We have to catch up to them!"

What's wrong with her?

I ran ahead, not caring if Jojo heard me or not. My heart thumped so hard it felt like it would burst in my chest. I had to get to the taxi at all costs. But before I could reach it, it rolled through the gate and into the cemetery.

Jojo came up panting behind me. "They might be headed for Tiger's place."

"Do you know where it is?" I asked, trying to catch my breath.

Jojo nodded to the left. "Yeah. He lives in a fancy grave house in the Chinese cemetery."

He spat the words out as if they left a bad taste in his mouth, his lips pursed into a thin, grim line. With nostrils flaring, he stared after the vehicle and the man inside who had beaten his friend to death. It was too late for Teddy, but not for Mama.

"What are we waiting for? Let's follow the taxi." Before I could break into a run, Jojo grabbed my arm, pulling me back. I tried to break free but his grip held strong. "Let go of me!"

"Hang on a minute!" His large eyes stared down at me until I stopped struggling. "Tiger's gang will see us coming. It'll be like walking into a cage of angry monkeys, too dangerous. We'll take a shortcut."

Danger was the last thing on my mind. I had to admit, though, that Jojo was right. "Where is it?"

The shortcut was not inside the cemetery. Jojo and I ran down Bonifacio Avenue, keeping close to the outer wall, toward Merced Street. The sky was overcast, the air hot and still.

"I found a small passage through this fence a couple of years ago." Jojo puffed out each word while he ran beside me. "It leads right into the Chinese cemetery."

I didn't see the gate until Jojo stopped in front of it. It was rectangular and small, only as high as my waist. The metal door had the letters *PPC*, Philippine Power Corporation, engraved along the top. It didn't have a handle.

Jojo dropped to his knees, running his fingers along the edges of the door. Did he remember how to open it? *Hurry. Hurry.* My heart pounded out the rhythm of the word. I couldn't stand still. I got down on my knees to feel the edges for something, anything, to open the gate.

Jojo's fingers paused at the top corner and pulled a metal bolt to the right. He pushed the door open and crawled through. I crawled in after him, almost climbing over him to get to the other side.

We were inside a small caged area. A humming metal box stood in the center, with sheets of corrugated metal over our heads. We couldn't climb the chain-link barrier because the space between it and the roof was too narrow.

"How are we going to get through the fence?"

"By crawling under it."

Jojo crouched alongside the wire mesh. He pulled and bent it upward. "This fence was meant to keep out animals and birds, not people," he said with a smirk, and waved his hand at the hole he made. "Ladies first!"

The edge of the fence raked across my back as I crawled through. I had never been to this part of the cemetery before. It was like walking into a different place, a different time. Here, the resident dead were housed in monuments of marble and glass, guarded by gold-and-red lacquered dragons.

"They look more like mansions than grave houses," I whispered. It was so quiet that our voices seemed to echo between the mausoleums.

Some of the buildings were two stories high, complete with windows, steps, and doors painted with red-and-gold trim. Some of the entryways were made of glass. You could see into tiled rooms with gleaming marble tombs and oiled brass grave markers. I even glimpsed a glass table with matching chairs topped with a vase of fresh lilies. If this was how they housed their dead, I couldn't even imagine what the living had for homes. Jojo and I were the only people here. No squatters.

"I know what you're thinking. The grave houses here look too fancy just to bury someone inside them. My grandmother used to wash clothes for a Chinese family when I was little. She learned that they bury their dead this way because they believed that death was a continuation of life, and that their afterlife should mirror how they lived on earth. She told me there was a Chinese philosopher who said, 'treat death as life.'" Jojo sniffed, then shrugged.

I nodded as if I understood. But really I didn't. It seemed like such a waste. Papa's mausoleum was a simple one and had been in his family for years.

"Come on, let's find that taxi."

"This way." Jojo grabbed hold of my hand and pulled me up the street. His fingers felt hot in mine. I held on tight, glad that he was with me. Our slippers made a gentle slapping sound as we ran. The drumming of my heart grew and filled my ears. I also heard the low thrumming of an idling car. It came from a street ahead of us.

The taxi was parked behind another car in front of a large grave house with two floors. The walls were white. They glittered in the sun. Jojo said the builders probably mixed crushed glass in the cement to give that effect. This one had columns supporting a covered porch. On either side of the door stood stone lion statues, mouths open, as if to frighten away anyone who would disturb the dead inside. Curtains fluttered in the windows on the second floor like waving flags. Was Mama inside the building or still in the taxi?

I tugged on Jojo's hand. "We have to get closer."

We ran down the street, then ducked behind a low wall when the gate of the grave house opened and two men came outside. One them was Tiger, smoking a cigarette. The other one was large, with dark, pockmarked skin and a wide, bulbous nose. He was dressed in black pants, a pressed shirt, and leather shoes. He carried a leather bag with papers sticking out of it.

"Trust me, sir, she's not going to forget to pay her debt next time," said Tiger.

The man nodded. He chuckled and glanced at his watch. "Make sure the other grave rats who owe me money know that they either pay or work in the factory. Well, if my calculations are correct, she worked more than enough hours to pay her debt. I'm not completely heartless, so I will pay her for the additional work she did. Here is your allowance, plus a little extra." The man handed Tiger an envelope. "I want you to give the first floor a fresh coat of paint. And tell your hooligans to stop sleeping on top of the tombs. My wife will kick you all out if she finds out you're disrespecting her family."

The man walked over to the taxi and also handed an envelope to Mama, who was still sitting in the backseat. She sat up, ran her hand through her hair, and nodded at whatever the man was saying. Without another word, the big man got into his car and left. Tiger flicked his cigarette into the street and leaned into the open door of the taxi.

"Ma—" I started to scream. Tiger's head whipped in our direction. Jojo covered my mouth and pulled me down. His eyes pleaded for me to be quiet.

The soft thud of footsteps came toward us. My chest thundered with fear. I wanted to move, to run, but my body stayed frozen in place. The footsteps stopped, then moved away again. Jojo loosened his grip on me and I inhaled a deep, shuddering breath of relief.

He leaned over, cupped his mouth to my ear, and said, "We'll have to stay hidden. If he catches us, we're dead."

We listened to Tiger's fading footsteps. A car door slammed. The taxi's engine revved and hummed. Then it rolled away down the street.

"Come on," said Jojo. We ran after it as fast as our slippers allowed. We were almost to my alley when I noticed someone struggling to stand by the side of the road.

Mama. I ran to her. My throat ached at how she trembled, fighting to steady herself.

"Mama!" I wrapped my arms around her waist, tears stinging my eyes. She could barely keep her head up. Her lips moved but no sound came from them.

"Let's go home, Mama."

Jojo and I held her between us so she could walk, but she was too weak.

"Come on, let's get her on my back," said Jojo.

With my hands under Mama's armpits, I pushed her over Jojo's shoulders. She moaned softly but didn't protest. He crouched in front of her, catching her weight on his back. I held on to her while Jojo stood up. He pulled up her knees with each hand and leaned forward to keep steady. Mama's thin body was so light that it startled me. *When was the last time she ate?*

I stared at her pale face, rocking against Jojo's shoulder as we walked home.

What happened to you, Mama?

Chapter Sixteen

Mama lay on the woven mat in our grave house, still as death. The only sign of life was the gentle rise and fall of her chest. A single candle burned in the corner. It gave the grave house and everything in it a comforting, warm, orange glow.

Jojo had sat by the door all day, answering questions for the curious and concerned in my cemetery neighborhood. He had his head down on his arms now, probably as exhausted as I was. My eyes ached but I couldn't sleep.

"Jo." His head shot up, startled, when I placed my hand on his arm. He grabbed hold of it; his bloodshot eyes darted between me and where Mama lay.

"Is everything okay? What happened?"

"She's sleeping." My hand twisted in his and held it. I remembered how at first I hadn't even wanted to be his friend. Now, it was like having an older brother. More than I deserved, considering how mean I had been to him when I first came to live in the cemetery.

Jojo rubbed his eyes and fought to stay awake. I squeezed his hand again. "Hey, why don't you go home? Mama and I will be fine for now. Your grandmother must be worried sick about you."

"No, she's not worried. I sent little Ernie with a message for her. She knows I'm here. I'll go home if you want me to."

"Oh, no. It's just—well, I'll have to help my mother with—uh, you know." My hand waved toward a bucket in the corner.

"Say no more!" He stood up and smoothed his shirt down, his eyes darting away from the bucket. I didn't mean to embarrass him, but I would need a little privacy later on. For Mama and for myself.

"Do you think you could come back tomorrow? With your grandmother?" I glanced at Mama's hollow face, her sunken eyes and cheeks. I was going to need his grandmother's help in case Mama got worse.

"We'll be here." He gave me an encouraging smile, patted me on the shoulder, and then left. I hoped they would come back, though a little voice inside of me told me not to depend on it, that I had to try and figure out what to do on my own.

It was nearly dawn. My eyes and my body ached, but I was too afraid to go to sleep. With my chin resting against my knees, I listened to Mama breathe.

I couldn't take my eyes from her, too afraid to look away and find that I had imagined her. *She is home. She didn't leave me.*

It had been a long time since I had felt Mama's embrace. I had the sudden urge to touch her, to feel close to her again. Under the kulambo, I curled into a ball and snuggled against her back. Mama's warmth filled me with longing for what we both had lost, and what we both needed to have once again.

My eyes drifted to the shadowy outline of my sweet potato plant and its drooping stems. My thoughts grew vague, distant.

I closed my eyes and let the darkness take me far, far away.

I woke up with sweat beaded on my forehead and nose.

It felt like I was leaning on a bundle of clothes left out in the sun too long. I thought it was the heat that woke me, but it wasn't. It was Mama's moans. She turned her head, her face tight with pain as she clutched her belly. Her hair looked wild and matted against the makeshift pillow under her head. She moaned again when I brushed the hair from her face. The papery softness of her skin was dry and hot.

"Mama?"

No answer. She was radiating heat like a stove. I'd thought only children had fevers. I tried to remember what Mama did whenever I had one. I got up to find some cloth and a basin of water.

With a thin, wet towel, I wiped down Mama's arms and legs, then covered her forehead with it. I fanned her with a piece of cardboard. It was the only other thing I could think of doing to cool her fever.

I was getting ready to sponge her down again when I noticed a spot of blood on her dress. I touched the smudge and it blossomed into a bigger stain. *What?* Where was the blood coming from? I bit my fist to keep from crying. I was too afraid to look but I knew I had to. My hands trembled when I lifted the edge of her dress and took a peek.

Mama had scratches and insect bites all over her arms and legs. Right above her hip was a raised lump about the size of a baseball. Pus and blood dripped from a torn scab on top of the swollen wound. Pink streaks radiated from it like a sunburst. Mama had had boils before, but never anything this bad.

The man in the nice clothes had said that Mama had been working in a factory. She smelled like she hadn't bathed or changed for days.

What am I going to do? I squeezed my eyes shut. I had to calm down and think.

The first thing to do was to clean her up. When I was little and I had a fever, Mama would give me a sponge bath. I rummaged through our baskets and pulled out a fresh duster and underwear. At the bottom of one was a small bottle of rubbing alcohol. It was only half full. With a fresh basin of water, I poured what was left of the alcohol and mixed it in with my finger.

My mother had done the same for our old neighbor Aling Lily when she came home from the hospital after an operation. She used to take me with her since Papa was at work. I remember watching Mama change the old woman's clothes and clean her wound. Now it was my turn to do the same for my mother.

Mama stirred and moaned as I undressed her and wiped her down. When I tried to clean the pus out of her wound, she cried out.

"I'm sorry, Mama."

Tears rolled down her dry, hot cheeks. She whispered, "That's okay, anak. I've had that boil for a while now. It just won't heal. I don't understand what can be making me feel so sick."

I covered the swollen lump on her hip with a clean, thin towel. There was nothing more to be done about it for now but to wait for Lola Mercy. She would know what to do.

After I dressed her, Mama peered at me through half-open eyes. She licked her dry lips, lifted her hand to my cheek, and said, "Nora."

Her hand was so hot. I pressed it to my face, wetting it with my tears. Her eyes pooled with moisture. She blinked, sending rivulets down her cheeks. She tried to turn herself, to lie on her side, but her face tightened in pain.

"What happened to you, Mama? I've been worried for days."

She licked her lips and whispered, "Water."

Mama slowly lifted herself onto her elbow and drank from the cup I held to her lips. She lowered herself down, lines of pain etched across her face again. "Can we talk later? I feel so tired."

Her eyes closed and her breathing steadied. I looked at the empty bottle of rubbing alcohol lying on the floor by the basin. There was a drugstore right across the street from Aling Lydia's home where I could buy more. Maybe the lady who ran the store could tell me what medicine I could buy to help Mama's pain. I still had some of the money Aling Lydia had paid me. Maybe I could make a quick trip while Mama rested. It would be better to have someone here to watch over her while I was gone. Were Jojo and Lola Mercy still coming over?

Still undecided over whether to go or stay, I sat on the mat and stared at the concrete floor. There were a couple of ants moving across it, each carrying a crumb of food. In a way, squatters were a lot like them. We scavenged for what we needed to survive, just like ants. We lived in a sort of colony, like ants. We shared food and protected one another. A single ant couldn't live by itself, but in a colony, it would survive, just as Mama and I had endured here in the cemetery. Tiger was also a squatter, but he wasn't an ant. He was a cockroach.

The purple-and-green leaves of my sweet potato plant

looked dry, and had curled along the edges from thirst. I sprinkled a little water into the pot. It wasn't enough. I'd have to water it when I returned from the drugstore.

I stood up and looked outside. Maybe Aling Nena could look after Mama while I went to the store. It wouldn't be for long anyway.

After setting up the kulambo over Mama to keep the flies and mosquitoes away, I made sure the bars were covered with a sheet to shield her from prying eyes.

The alley was busy as usual; the voices of playing children and scolding mothers sounded strangely comforting to me. I took one last look at Mama before stepping outside. What if she woke up looking for me? What if Aling Nena was too busy to check on Mama? But I had to buy the medicine soon in case she needed it. I was closing the gate of the grave house when I heard a sweet singsong voice coming from up the alley.

"Nora, where are you going?" called Lola Mercy as she shuffled over. She pointed to the basket over her other arm. "I've brought something for your mother. Let me have a look at her."

My fellow ants had arrived.

Chapter Seventeen

JOJO HADN'T COME OVER LIKE HE PROMISED HE WOULD. He'd told me yesterday that he'd be here but Lola Mercy said he was off doing his water chores. And he also had a tomb-painting job later in the day. He had to do something to make money, right? His grandmother depended on him. But still, I missed him.

"Let me have a look at your mother," said Lola Mercy as she crawled beneath the kulambo. She began to unpack what she had in her basket. "Did you have somewhere to go, Nora? I'll look after your mother until you come back."

I nodded, relieved that Mama was in safe hands. Before I left, I counted the money I had. It would be enough for a few days of medicine and food at the most. I could sell garlands, but who would take care of Mama? It seemed too much to keep asking Lola Mercy or Aling Nena to help out. I wouldn't be able to repay them.

The drugstore stood on the opposite corner of Aling Lydia's house and the bakery. A wall-to-wall glass counter and display case ran through the whole establishment, containing ointments, creams, and even cosmetics. Two young women were busy with other customers so I waited. I held my money, the bills folded lengthwise, so they could see that I was here to buy something, that I wasn't just standing around ogling the items inside the display case.

I glanced across the street at the bakery. I thought about the job Aling Lydia had offered me, the day I was late to do the washing and she had hired someone else to take my place. A lump of bitterness rose up in my chest, remembering how I had shouted and cried, and that I had run away instead of accepting the job. Would she still take me on to help out in the bakery? Maybe I could ask her for a loan and work it off.

No, she won't. She'll chase you out with a broom before you have a chance to speak. I shuffled my feet, my stomach queasy. I should go and talk to Aling Lydia. I had to try, for Mama's sake.

One of the young women finished with her customer and shifted her attention to me. She walked over to where I stood and asked, "How can I help you?"

I told her about Mama's boil and the pain she was in. She looked at how much money I had and said I could afford a few foil-wrapped packets of aspirin and penicillin. She told me that since I could only afford a few tablets of the antibiotic, I should crush the tablet into a powder and press it into Mama's wound. There was also enough money to buy the supplies I needed to keep it clean. I paid her and told her I would be back to pick up the items.

Before I could lose my nerve, I crossed the street to Aling Lydia's house. I stopped at the gate and listened, debating if I should ring the buzzer on the wall or just march through and knock on their front door.

The decision was made for me when Perla strode out of the house. She was wearing shorts and a T-shirt that said *I ♥ NY* on the front. She didn't see me until she crossed the courtyard to the back door of the bakery. She paused with a hand on one hip and gazed at me, her long, straight, side-parted hair covering one eye. Then she sauntered over to the gate, tucking a strand behind her ear.

Be brave. "Hi, Perla. Is your mother home?" My voice came out too soft.

Perla made a face and tilted her head. "What?"

I swallowed the dry lump in my throat. "Is your mother home? I want to ask her something."

"No. She's out for the rest of the afternoon. My mother is very busy, you know." She turned to walk back to the bakery.

"Wait!"

Perla spun around, arms crossed in front of her chest, her eyebrows raised.

I swallowed again. "Can you please give her a message for me?"

She rolled her eyes and sighed. "What is it?"

"Can you tell her that I found my mother and that she's sick and if I can still have the job to sweep the bakery so I can buy her medicine," I said in one breath. I stared at her Hello Kitty slippers the whole time because looking at her face would make me not want to talk. I murmured, "Salamat," and hurried back across the street to the drugstore. I stole a glance behind me. Perla was gone. My stomach fell. She wouldn't give her mother the message. Why would she?

The woman at the drugstore filled a plastic bag with a few sachets of individually wrapped painkillers and penicillin, alcohol, and bandages. On the way home, the aroma of chicken-rice porridge drew me to a food stand. But all I could afford was the plain one, no chicken. It would have to do. At another stand, I bought some bananas and eggs.

When I arrived at the grave house, Lola Mercy was feeding Mama some brown liquid with a spoon. I let out a sigh, grateful that she was around to help. I used to feel bad that I never knew my grandmothers. I didn't feel that way now.

"How is she, Lola?" Mama's eyes were closed, but the crease between her brows was gone. I felt like a swimmer coming up for air after spending too much time underwater. It felt good to see Mama looking more comfortable.

"Her fever is down, but she's not out of trouble yet," said

Lola. She blinked a few times and her frown deepened as she covered and set aside the jar that contained the brown liquid. "I've been feeding her this tea I made from my stash of lagundi leaves. Just a couple of spoonfuls every fifteen minutes for an hour usually does the trick."

Lola seemed to want to say more. Something was bothering her. It felt as if I was plunged underwater again, unable to breathe. The silence was suddenly thick with dread. I waited for Lola to speak.

"Anak, I hope you don't mind. I noticed the stain on your mother's clothes so I checked to see what was causing it. I've seen boils before, but this one looks bad. There are pink streaks spreading away from it, and the surrounding skin is very swollen and hot. You have to consider taking her to a hospital if her fever continues and her pain gets worse."

"Hospital?"

Lola patted my hand, but it didn't prevent the panic rising in my throat like vomit. How would that be possible? The money I had left was barely enough for food, and would last maybe another week at most. It was out of the question to look for a job right now while Mama was sick. "Is there a chance that the infection will go away on its own?"

"Maybe. If you keep her wound very clean. We will have to wait and see." When Lola said the word "clean," I remembered the bags I held in my hand. Yes, I could do that. Lola stood to go. Her face, though, never lost that puckered look around her eyes and mouth. She was still worried. But Mama looked comfortable for now. I felt more hopeful than afraid.

"Thank you, Lola, for staying with Mama. Please take some bananas and eggs."

"Please keep the food for yourself and your mother. You're going to need your strength if your mother is going to get through this. Now listen, my dear. When your mother wakes up, give her more of the lagundi tea. Then give her something to eat. The stronger she is, the better it will be for her."

She took my hands into both of hers, which felt dry and papery. They were brown, gnarled, but strong. "We can only put our trust in God to keep us safe. Pray the Rosary. It will help calm your nerves. If you run out of the tea, or if you need me to come back, just let Jojo know when he comes around." Lola squeezed my hand one more time. She leaned in and whispered, "It's a good time to call your uncle, just in case."

"I will. Salamat po," I whispered back, and watched her hobble away.

"Nora." Mama's voice was so soft I wasn't sure she had spoken at all. I went over and knelt beside her. My body ached and felt heavy. I needed to eat and sleep but my mind said it was time to take care of Mama.

Her eyes fluttered open when I pressed my cheek to her forehead to check for fever. I had seen Lola do this to Jojo when they came to pick up their laundry some time ago. I'd asked her why she didn't use her hand and she said that the cheek was more sensitive to warmth. She was right. The heat from Mama's forehead was intense. I could still feel it after I moved away.

Mama watched me as I soaked the rag in cool water and placed it back on her forehead. "Have some more of this tea, Mama. It's supposed to help your pain and fever. Here, Mama, take these too."

I tore open a packet of aspirin and penicillin and gave her one of each. The lady at the pharmacy had told me to crush the antibiotic, but it seemed to me that it would be better if Mama swallowed it instead.

"Thank you, anak," said Mama, her voice soft and whispery like rustling palm trees in the wind. With a grimace, she raised herself on one elbow, placed the pills on her tongue, and sipped the tea from a spoon. She clutched at her side as she lowered herself down again.

Was it the right time to ask her where she had been? Was Mama strong enough to answer? I had to know. I deserved to know. The loneliness and abandonment I had felt flashed through my mind. My hands balled into fists.

"What happened to you, Mama? Where did you go?" Unwanted tears trickled down my face. Mama tried to brush them off my cheek but I turned away. I didn't want her to touch me just then. "I waited for you! Then I tried to find you. And when I didn't, I found debts and Tiger."

She looked at me, with squinted eyes at first, and then they flew wide open. "You mean you didn't know where I was? Didn't you get my message?"

"What?"

"I asked Mr. Santiago to send a message. He promised me that someone would be sent to tell you where I was." Mama blinked as tears welled up in her eyes. She stretched her hand out to me, grabbed hold of my hand, and squeezed tight. "Anak, please let me explain."

I unclenched my fists and wrapped her hand in both of mine. I could see my exhaustion mirrored in Mama, only ten times worse. I should have let her rest, but if she was ready to talk, then I was prepared to listen.

"Oh, Nora. I want so much more for you than this. I want you to go to school and have a real chance at making a good life for yourself. It was what your father would've wanted. I was desperate and made some terrible mistakes. You know about my debts."

My heart felt heavy. "Was that why you went back to see Lola Fely?"

"How do you know about that?"

"Jojo and I went to see Rosie, to find out if she knew where you were and what happened to you. She told me you were upset when you returned from a visit with Lola Fely. She also told me about Mr. Santiago and Tiger."

Mama grimaced and remained silent for a moment. "Yes, that's true. I didn't understand why I hadn't heard from my brother—"

"Wait, I have something to show you." I remembered Tito Danny's letter. I pulled it out of my pocket and showed it to her.

She sighed after reading it and gave it back to me. "Well, it wasn't the news I'd hoped for, but all the same, I'm so relieved to finally hear from him. When he didn't answer my previous letters, I began worrying that something had happened to him. So I thought maybe, just maybe, Lola Fely could lend us the cash we needed to pay off my debts and boat fare for us so we could finally go home. I was wrong."

My skin crawled at the thought of Mama groveling at Lola Fely's feet. Especially since she had never returned the money Mama "invested" in her dry goods store scheme. It should've been her last resort to go crawling back to Lola Fely. It probably was.

"I should've stayed away. She's a terrible woman. It's hard to believe she's Papa's aunt. She was all bitterness about your father's watch, and insisted that if we wanted to borrow money, we had to give her the watch to keep until we repaid our debt. As if she'd really give it back. She just wanted a reason to get her hands on it." Mama chuckled a little at the memory and then grimaced with pain. She motioned for more tea.

Papa's watch. How was I going to tell her that we didn't have it anymore? That Tiger had taken it?

Mama closed her eyes and said, "I wasn't going to let that bruha have the watch. When Rosie told me about Mr. Santiago, I decided to borrow money. I hoped my luck would change and I could double it. Then we would have enough to settle all my debts and start a new life in Davao."

Mama took a deep breath. "A few days ago, I was play-ing mahjong with Rosie at her friend's house where the stakes were high. When Tiger showed up, he insisted I come with him and talk to his boss, Mr. Santiago. Rosie didn't want me to go but I knew I had to. I didn't want to cause Rosie's friend any trouble. She wanted to go with me but Tiger refused. I told Rosie I'd call her. But the factory didn't have a working telephone." She paused. "Give me a sip of water, anak."

I helped her take a few sips. "What did Mr. Santiago want to talk to you about?"

"What else?" She half-snorted. "I had missed two pay-ments and he wanted to know why. I promised he would have his money soon but he wouldn't let me leave. He wanted me to make good on the loan by working for him in his T-shirt factory."

Mama was quiet for a while. Then she said, "I wanted to go home and tell you about it and make arrangements with Lola Mercy to look after you, but they wouldn't let me. I asked Mr. Santiago to send you a message."

"I never got it." That was probably why Tiger had been here the first day Mama disappeared. I wasn't ready to tell her about that, either. Why upset her more than necessary? "Was that where you got all these insect bites?"

"Yes. The building had lots of mosquitoes. They kept me working for three straight days with very few breaks. There was food and a place to sleep but I wanted to get my work done as soon as possible and come home." Her lips curled into a smile. "I made three times my quota, more than enough to repay Mr. Santiago. He is a fair man and paid me for the extra work."

That must have been what I saw the man give to Mama yesterday. "Well, it's a good thing we have the money. Lola said that if your fever didn't go away, I would have to take you to the hospital."

Suddenly, Mama's eyes grew big and her hands patted at her dress. "Where is it? Where is it?"

"Where is what, Mama?"

"There should be a folded envelope in my pocket."

I scrambled over to the basket that held our dirty clothes. I pulled out the dress Mama had been wearing and looked for the pocket. There it was, a folded white envelope stamped with Mr. Santiago's name and the address of his store.

But the envelope was empty.

Chapter Eighteen

MAMA COULD NOT STOP CRYING. I WOULD HAVE BEEN just as inconsolable if I wasn't busy trying to calm her down. Her sobs escalated to screams that brought curious neighbors peering through the gaps in the sheet that covered the bars of our grave house. Mama even struggled to stand and said over and over that she had to talk to Mr. Santiago. She wanted me to call a tricycle, anything that would get her to him so she could ask—no, demand—he tell her what happened to the money.

Mama hobbled as far as the alley and collapsed. When she clasped her side, it came away reddish and smelly, with fresh blood and pus. Aling Nena fussed over Mama as she helped me bring her back inside. I expected her to fire questions at me, but she didn't. Her eyes grew big at the sight of blood and she left us alone, shooing away the other spectators that had gathered.

Mama lay on the mat, unmoving. She gazed at the ceiling, her eyes glistening with moisture. Her hands lay still. I pressed them against my cheek.

How much more could we suffer? Resentment bubbled up inside me. *If only she hadn't borrowed money! Stupid gambling!* But all Mama wanted was to make a better life for us, right? Sure, she made mistakes, some really bad ones. If she felt cheated, then I did too. Cheated out of having a home and a father. Cheated by people who thought we were too stupid and poor to care. Cheated by Lola Fely out of Papa's savings, which Mama had invested in her business scam. Cheated by Tiger out of the only legacy my father had left us, that could have saved us from starvation. Cheated by Mr. Santiago out of the money that could've given Mama a chance to see a doctor.

Mama pulled me onto her shoulder. We cried together for what seemed like hours. "Mama, what are we going to do?"

"I have to talk to Mr. Santiago. Perhaps there was some mistake and he gave me the wrong envelope. He said something to me in the taxi but I don't remember what it was. Don't worry, anak, I'll take care of it when I'm stronger." Mama's voice was hoarse from crying. She gave me a weak squeeze around my shoulders and let go.

After I changed her bandages and helped her into some

fresh clothes, I went next door and asked Tina if I could boil the eggs on her portable stove. Her grave house happened to have an electric plug. After they were cooked, I gave her a couple and went home. Mama and I shared the porridge and a couple of the bananas and hard-boiled eggs. The bitterness of the lagundi tea made Mama grimace but she drank it with her medicines without complaint. Her skin was still feverish and I wondered how much of the tea she would have to drink to make the fever go away. I wanted to believe that it would be all she needed to get better. But I had a feeling that she would need more.

I remembered when Papa had cut himself while fixing a window and how the cut became swollen and smelly. He went to the doctor at Mama's insistence and came home with some medicine in a tube that he had to spread on the cut in the morning and again at night. Would Mama need something like that? If she did, then we would need more money. Would Perla give her mother my message? Would Aling Lydia let me work in the bakery like she said she would? Probably not, especially after the way I had behaved. The memory of it made me cringe again and again. There was only one other way for me to make money. I would have to go out and sell my everlasting-daisy garlands. But that would mean leaving Mama alone, and I wasn't sure I could do that. I took out my bag of flowers, a needle, and some thread. The only noise in the grave house was the rustle of dry petals and Mama's breathing.

"Papa, can you hear me? I wish you were here. Tell me

what to do. Tell me what to do," I whispered, piercing my needle through daisy after daisy until the chain was long enough to tie the ends together.

I pressed my cheek against the cool cement of my father's tomb and felt the heat in my face drain away. It calmed me.

The answer came to me then. Lola Mercy had suggested I call my uncle. I lay the garland I had finished down on top of a few others. Inside one of the baskets, I found Mama's notebook, the one she'd told me not to touch. I glanced at Mama's face to make sure she was sleeping. The paper squeaked against the wire spirals. The edges of the notebook looked a little warped, and it smelled like wet cardboard. The pages were filled with doodles, addresses, phone numbers, and—a list of her debts. *That's why she didn't want me to look at this.* I stared at the list. The entry at the top was a name I didn't recognize. Mama had borrowed a hundred pesos and next to it, the date she paid it back. The first few entries were that way. The rest of them had no payback date. The very last name on the list read *Tiger/Santiago.*

I squeezed my eyes shut, trying to erase the image from my mind. It didn't work. The memory of the empty envelope followed it. I flipped to the next page, rustling the paper so hard I was sure Mama would wake up. I ran my finger down the list and found what I had been looking for.

As quietly as possible, I tore a page out from the back of the notebook. Using the pen Mama kept inside the spiral binding, I wrote down Tito Danny's phone number.

Mama's face looked serene while she slept, except for the

slight crease between her brows—the only sign of her discomfort. I could probably ask Mang Rudy if I could use his cell phone, and then sell a few garlands. I'd be back when she woke up.

I hung my gold-and-pink everlasting-daisy garlands on my arm, the page of notebook paper clutched between my fingers. With my free hand, I drew back the sheet covering the door, glancing one more time at Mama's sleeping face.

What if she grew weaker instead of stronger? How would I be able to leave her to find work? I could go see Aling Lydia but I wouldn't be able to face Perla again. There had to be something else I could do, a job I could get, but what? Who would hire a dark skinny girl like me with clothes that screamed "squatter"?

Maybe I should try speaking to Aling Lydia, no matter how embarrassed it made me. The humiliation would be worth it, if it meant that I could take Mama to the doctor. If only I still had Papa's watch, then at least I would have something to pawn. I stamped my foot, cursing Tiger under my breath.

My toe nudged the bucket where my sweet potato plant grew. Its dry, drooping stems shivered. It had to stay alive and grow. Mama would need this food to get stronger. I watered it and moved it to a spot where it would catch more sunlight.

It was time to go. Out of the corner of my eye, an indistinct shape seemed to hover on the other side of the kulambo that covered Mama. The hair on my neck and arms rose as if a cold breeze brushed against me.

"Papa?" But the shadow continued to hover. My voice came out in strangled whisper. "I know that you watch over us. Please look after Mama when I leave to go out and sell these flowers. And Papa? Please ask God to send us a miracle."

I looked for the shadow. It was gone. Was it just my imagination? I wanted to believe that it wasn't.

Hidden behind the Santo Niño was a small bowl holding a short stubby candle. I set it in front of the statue and lit it, mumbling a prayer to make Mama well and to ease Papa's restless spirit.

After closing the gate, I walked over to Mang Rudy's grave house to see if he was home. He wasn't. So I asked Aling Nena to check in on Mama before setting out for the main cemetery gate. It was Friday afternoon. Visitors might be looking for garlands. I had ten of them and I hoped to sell every single one.

Up ahead, Kuya Efren was loading books, paper, and pencils onto his pushcart classroom. He stacked the school supplies on shelves under the chalkboard and began folding his plastic mats. He looked up just as I passed him.

"Nora! We missed you in class today." He smiled, waving me over. "Have you had a chance to read the book of folktales I gave to you?"

I hesitated, then moved closer. "Sorry po, I haven't. I had to work. My mom is sick and she needs medicine," I said, patting my armload of garlands. "I'll come another time."

"Sorry to hear about your mother. I hope she will be well soon, so you can come to class." He flipped the side cover over. "By the way, I have something special for you today," said Kuya Efren, handing me an unfamiliar paperback book. He smiled down at me, crinkling his eyes at the corners.

The title on the cover read *6th Grade Reviewer*. The pages were filled with math problems, Filipino, and social studies exercises. A slip of yellow paper fell out. Kuya picked it up, smoothed it open, handed it to me, and said, "Go on, read it!"

It was a flier about St. Anne's Academy. My eyes scanned the advertisement.

St. Anne's Priory, located at the St. Anne's Academy campus. The sisters would like to invite girls between the ages of five and fourteen to apply for this year's St. Anne's Academic Scholarship for deserving girls in need. The scholarship includes tuition and books. Along with instruction and prayer, candidates will participate in the care and maintenance of the convent. Applications are now open.

I looked up at Kuya. "I don't understand. This is about scholarships. I'm not in school right now. Don't you need good grades to win one of these?"

Kuya tapped a finger on the paper in my hand. "This is a different kind. St. Anne's gives a scholarship to a deserving child in need every year. You have an edge because you've only missed a year of school and you deserve to keep going.

All you need is a recommendation, which I will give you. Then all you have to do is take an entrance exam."

"A test?" I frowned, staring down at the paper. The letters began to swirl and tumble before my eyes. Was it true? Could I really go back to school? "I don't know if I can pass it."

Kuya laughed. "Don't worry! Just work through the book I gave you. If you have questions, I will be here every Friday afternoon and on the weekends. The test is still a couple of months away so there is enough time to prepare."

He gave me tips on how to use the book and told me to do at least one exercise a day.

I sighed, glancing down at the garlands hanging from my arm. It was time to go.

"Salamat po, Kuya, for the book and for telling me about the scholarship."

"Walang anuman." He handed me a canvas bag with his Outreach Education on Wheels logo printed on both sides. "Here, you can have this bag to carry your book in. There are forms from St. Anne inside. I've filled out the recommendation form and signed it. Just have your mother fill out the permission forms before the test date."

"Thanks again, Kuya." I slipped the book and pencil inside and shouldered the bag. The everlasting daisies made a soft scratching noise on the canvas as they swung back and forth on my arm. A warm bubble of hope settled in my stomach.

I could go to school.

I didn't want to think about it now but I couldn't help myself.

My excitement made me walk faster. I would tell Mama about it as soon as she got better. *And she will get better.* No matter how many garlands I had to make and sell, I would do it. And maybe, when she was strong enough, she could meet Kuya Efren and he would help her find work again.

Visitors at the cemetery gates came in at a steady stream. The garlands sold out in just a couple of hours.

The secret pocket at my waist sagged with coins and bills. It was time to go home. I passed through the gate, counting out some of the change. One of the squatters had a little sari-sari store, where they sold some candy, snacks, and soda. I wanted to buy Mama her favorite orange drink as a surprise treat. One of the coins fell and rolled away into a bush just inside the gate. I ran after it, squeezing between rough branches and leaves. When I bent to pick up the stray coin I noticed a low bush with glossy leaves and small white flowers growing between two tombs. Sampaguita. Mama's favorite jasmine blossom. I formed a little basket with the front end of my shirt and collected as much as it could hold.

I was cradling my harvest, trying to squeeze through the gap in the bushes, when I noticed a group of loud-mouthed men coming through the gate. It was the bowlegged one I recognized first. *Tiger and his gang!* I dropped into a squat behind the bush. *Oh, please don't let them see me.* I kept my eyes squeezed shut as I muttered a quick prayer.

"Hey, boss! Where are we eating tonight?"

"Who do you think I am, your mother?"

It seemed like they were standing right next to me. I opened my eyes just a crack. I nearly gasped. Through the veil of bush leaves and branches, I saw Tiger crouched down tying the laces on a brand-new pair of sneakers. There was also a huge silver-and-black watch fastened to his wrist. Where did he get the money for new things?

A loud beep buzzed through the air. Tiger pulled a cell phone from his pocket and looked at it. He made a face, put the phone away, and continued tying his shoes.

"Looks like Mr. Santiago has a job for us tomorrow afternoon."

"It's about time! I've already run out of cash," said one of his thugs standing nearby. "Hey, boss. Those are some nice ladies' shoes."

"You better shut your mouth. What do you know about it, huh, crab legs?" Tiger got up and moved out of sight. *Whack!*

"Aray!" The taunting and chuckling faded as they moved away.

Tiger had a new watch. But what had he done with Papa's? Did he still have it? Would he give it back if I asked for it? It was crazy but possible. I mean, with his new watch, he wouldn't want Papa's old one anymore, would he? It made my insides twist at the thought of facing him again.

How could he take the watch from me and Mama, only to set it aside for something better? How did a cockroach like him get rewarded for doing bad things? It didn't seem fair. I worked hard, and for what? A mother who gambled away our money faster than we could make it? I pushed the ugly thought away. My mother was all I had left in the world. The money in my pocket would buy food but not much else. Medicine was expensive. I wanted Papa's watch back. I needed to have it back, but how?

My calves began to cramp. I was so caught up in my own thoughts I forgot that I was still squatting behind the bushes. After peeking through the leaves to make sure Tiger was gone, I stood. The heady scent of sampaguita engulfed me as I stretched. I must've crushed all the flowers I had collected while hiding. After a quick inspection, I found they were all good, the buds so fresh they popped back into the usual egg shape. I would make a necklace with them, hang it on my Santo Niño, and pray for a miracle. And I really needed one now.

On the way home, my anger still burned. What Tiger said about having a job to do tomorrow blazed in my mind. That meant he wasn't going to be home.

I could steal the watch back. I couldn't deny it was a crazy idea. A suicidal one, even. There were other possibilities to consider. I could swallow my pride and go to Aling Lydia again and ask if I could have the baking job so I could take Mama to the doctor. Maybe Kuya Efren could help me. Maybe Mama's fever would go away and her wound would heal. Maybe she'd straighten things out with Mr. Santiago and get the money he owed her.

Maybe not.

Chapter Nineteen

LOLA AND JOJO CAME OVER THE NEXT DAY WITH MORE lagundi tea and a pot of lugaw. I had some dried salted fish, which we crumbled over the hot rice porridge.

Mama sat up and ate a few spoonfuls. She pushed the bowl back into my hands. "Enough. I have to lie down."

"Give more of the tea, Nora. I'll be right back." Lola slurped up the last of her porridge, smacking her lips while she gathered the empty bowls. She shuffled out of the grave house to our water bucket to wash the dishes. Jojo followed to help.

I smoothed back Mama's hair away from her creased forehead. She hadn't slept well last night. We had run out of the tea and medicines. I pressed the edge of the cup to

Mama's lips. She gulped down a few mouthfuls and then lay back onto the mat. The pinched expression on her face began to relax. I rolled down the sides of the kulambo, arranging the folds around her.

If only I had reached Tito Danny last night. Mang Rudy had been home for a while when I returned from selling garlands. It was embarrassing, but I swallowed my discomfort and asked to use his cell phone. I offered to pay for the minutes I would use, but he had refused. I dialed Tito Danny's number, but there was no answer. I left a message, hoping the number was still correct.

Jojo came back with the basin of washed bowls and spoons. He nodded toward the bundles of everlasting-daisy garlands hanging from the grave house's black iron posts. "Hey, are you planning to go out there and sell these things today? I bet if you give me one of those bundles, I could sell it all in just one hour."

"There are over ten garlands in each bundle. It's impossible to sell them all in one hour."

"No, it isn't," said Jojo. The dimple in his cheek deepened.

"Yes, it is." I couldn't help but smile back at him. It was hard to argue with a boy who wore a sleeveless sky-blue shirt with the word *BABY* on the front in big pink letters.

Lola came shuffling back in at that moment, muttering to herself about useless grandsons. She sat next to me and leaned in close. "Since your mother is asleep, why don't you go and sell your flowers. I will stay with her."

"Thank you, Lola. I will." I kissed her soft, papery cheek.

Before I could stand up, she grabbed my arm and said in a stage whisper, "And take my pesky grandson with you."

Jojo tripped over my plant as we headed out the door. It nearly toppled to the ground. He patted the loosened dirt back down. I sighed, noticing how brown the leaves looked.

With each us of carrying a bundle of garlands, we walked to the main entrance of the cemetery, arguing over the best selling strategy. When we got there, Jojo positioned himself across the street from the gate. I stood on my usual spot just outside of it. Most of the time, I simply held out a garland to whoever passed by, hoping one of them would stop and buy one. An hour passed, and I had sold half of my flowers. I glanced across the street at Jojo. He was gone. He must've decided to move to another corner. Then I saw him walking through a throng of people empty-handed. He crossed the stream of traffic with a wide grin on his face.

"What happened? Where are the garlands?"

Jojo placed a wad of coins and bills into my open hand.

I stared at it in wonder. "How did you do that?"

"It was easy." He grabbed the rest of my garlands. He folded one into a crown and placed it on his head. "Watch this."

He walked into the throng, yelling, "EVER, EVERLASTING! EVER, EVERLASTING!"

I followed him through the crowds, taking payments

and making change for people who bought garlands from us. In half an hour, we had sold all of them, even the one on top of Jojo's head. We bought more aspirin and penicillin, along with some bread and cheese. I stopped to pick more sampaguita for my Santo Niño and then we headed home.

We saw Kuya Efren and his pushcart classroom parked on a street corner. I elbowed Jojo in the ribs.

"Do you like to read?"

"I would if I knew how." He scratched his head, trying not to look me in the eye. "Well, the truth is, Lola taught me enough so I could read signs and stuff. I can read comics, but I'm slow. I just look at the pictures mostly. I've never read a book."

I stopped walking. I swallowed the lump in my throat. "I know someone who could teach you. Come on."

I dragged Jojo to the pushcart classroom and introduced him to Kuya Efren. He gave Jojo a simple test to see how much he knew. Then he handed him a workbook with simple reading exercises. I volunteered to help him work through them. "Come to class with Nora. I hold class here three times a week. When you've answered all the questions, I'll give you a math lesson."

We waved goodbye and left. Out of the corner of my eye, I watched Jojo stare at the cover of the book with a frown.

I'd always wanted to ask him about what happened to his parents, and whether or not he had wanted to go to school, but I was too shy to ask. The bigger truth was, I was afraid that if I started asking him questions, he would start asking me about things I wasn't ready to talk about. Like about my father and how we ended up living in the cemetery. But at this moment, I didn't feel so afraid anymore. I already knew what had happened to his parents but the school part was still a mystery. "Can I ask you something?

Jojo glanced up from the book. He had been scrutinizing the cover page. "Sure."

"Did you ever want to go to school? You never mention it. If Mama and I had the money for uniforms, books, and supplies, I'd go back to school in a heartbeat." I gave him a sidelong glance. "I always wondered whether you ever did. I didn't want to offend you by asking. You don't have to answer it if you don't want to."

He shrugged. "What makes you think I'd mind? I've got nothing to hide. You have to stop being so uptight, Nora."

"What? Are you telling me I'm a snob? Do the other kids think so too?"

"No. Those are two different things. You're just serious most of the time. That's not the same as being a snob. Kids who live in the cemetery care and want the same things you do, but they're like me. They live day to day. We are happy to be alive, to have something to eat and a place to sleep. We say, bahala na! Come what may! It will be too depressing otherwise. Maybe the other kids keep their distance because you remind them of what they *should* be thinking about."

"Okay, so why do you hang around me? You don't seem to mind my seriousness." I nudged him. His eyes were still glued to the book and he almost tripped.

Jojo flipped to the next page. "You remind me of Teddy. He was serious like you. Always scheming for ways to make money. And you tell great stories." He jabbed my arm with his elbow. "And to answer your question, I do want to go to school, but I have to be realistic. I'm all my grandmother has, and she relies on me to take care of her. She's not as strong as she used to be. I actually did go to school when I was younger. Lola used to be a labandera, remember? That was when I was around seven years old. Anyway, she hurt her back and couldn't work anymore. Then she got sick with dengue fever. I had to stop going to school. I did odd jobs for a while. I fetched water or helped paint tombs before All Saints' Day. When Lola was better, I helped her roast corn outside the cemetery gates."

Bahala na. Come what may. Live for the day.

He snapped the book shut and tucked it under his arm. "Hey, are you serious about tutoring me?"

"Of course!"

"Are you going to be a strict teacher?"

"Absolutely. And you will be the best reader in the whole cemetery."

Jojo stared at me wide-eyed, frowning.

I laughed and punched him in the arm.

He rubbed it, pretending he was in pain. Then he poked me back. "Hey, want to go see something neat?"

"Sure." It wouldn't hurt to take a little detour on the way home. I thought about Mama and Lola Mercy waiting for us with a guilty pang. "Is it far? Your grandmother might be getting tired and I want to give my mother this medicine."

"Nah, it's really close. It will only take a few minutes." He nudged me again with his elbow. He grinned, his dark eyes glinting.

I sighed, grinning back. "Let's go."

We cut through a maze of tombs on our left and came out onto a smooth paved road. I had never been to this part of the cemetery before. It had clean, larger plots. Most of them had clipped grass growing around tombs of marble and a speckled stone Jojo called granite. There were also a few trees here. I didn't see any mausoleums, but some of the graves had a roof built over them to keep visitors out of the sun and rain. We passed a man holding a handkerchief over his mouth while he watched a couple of gravediggers. They were crouched in front of an open tomb, pulling out bones and laying them in a box. They would probably be placed back inside before the next burial.

Jojo made a right at the next corner. He opened a low gate and walked into a large grassy plot surrounded by a low brick wall. A cement path led to a marble platform at the center. On top of that stood a large pillar of stone.

Inside it, encased in glass, was a metal container with a sculpted base, handles, and cover. It looked old and fancy. I'd never seen anything like it.

"What is this place?"

"It's a grave." He pointed to the marble platform. A name had been engraved there in large block letters and the years of birth and death.

"Oh, so he's buried underneath. But what's the pillar for? And that metal thing inside it?" I pointed to the glass enclosure.

Jojo pushed my hand down. "It's not nice to point. The man is buried inside the urn. That's the container behind the glass. He was burned to ashes. Neat, huh? It's like becoming a piece of art when you die."

I would've elbowed him for scolding me but I didn't. All I could do was stare at the pillar and what lay inside it. The glass was greenish. A golden light shone above it, casting shadows on the designs carved into the urn. It was beautiful in a way that didn't make you feel sad, the way looking at an ordinary tomb would. It seemed like a nice place to just sit and think.

"You're right, it is like looking at art. Thanks for showing this to me. Maybe I'll bring Mama here to see it." I placed a few sampaguita flowers beneath the carved name on the platform, thinking about what a good and true friend Jojo had become. It was tempting to tell him about how I wanted to take back my father's watch, how I had thought about sneaking into Tiger's place to steal it. I wanted to tell him, but I couldn't risk it. If there was one thing I knew about Jojo, it was how he felt about Tiger. He would stop me.

I tugged on his arm. "Come on. It's time to go home."

❋

Jojo and his grandmother left after I insisted on sharing the bread and cheese with them. It was the least I could do. I offered to split the money with Jojo but he refused. I waved goodbye, promising Lola that I would let her know right away if Mama needed more of her special tea.

I lit a candle, setting it beside the burning mosquito coil. I crawled under the kulambo and lay on my stomach next to Mama. The book of folktales Kuya Efren had given to me lay on the mat. I flipped through the pages, trying to decide which story to read first.

"What are you reading?" asked Mama in a soft, sleepy voice.

"Just a book of Filipino folktales." I tilted the cover so she could see it.

"Is there one about the mango tree? That's my favorite."

I slid my finger down the table of contents. "Here's one! Would you like me to read it to you?"

Mama nodded, the crease between her eyebrows deepening, as if the simple movement caused her more pain.

Candlelight flickered over the pages. I began to read.

A TREE WITH NO NAME

THE LEGEND OF THE MANGO TREE

A Filipino Folktale

Once upon a time, in a sunny grove, in a valley of rolling green hills, stood a tree with no name.

The tree towered over all the others in the woodland, its trunk thick and sturdy, its leaves glossy green. It was magnificent to behold. The tree had no name because it bore no fruit.

Every morning, children would come to the thicket to harvest. They visited many trees there but not Tree-with-no-name.

They climbed Rambutan tree and picked its red, spiky fruit.

The children pranced to Tamarind tree and gathered its long brown pods for cooking.

They harvested the round, yellow-green, fragrant fruit of Guava tree.

The children left the grove with baskets overflowing.

The trees in the grove shook their branches and whispered, because all trees whisper.

"Oh my," sighed Guava tree. "That feels much better. My branches were so heavy with fruit that I could hardly keep my canopy up."

"I wish the children weren't so rough," whispered Rambutan tree. "My trunk is bruised and my branches are torn."

Tree-with-no-name listened and wondered. Filled with curiosity, it whispered to Tamarind tree, because all trees whisper.

"What is it like to have fruit? It seems wonderful."

"Yes, it is," whispered Tamarind tree. "But you will never understand, for you do not bear fruit. Truly, you do not belong with us."

Tree-with-no-name sighed. Some of its leaves drifted to the ground.

One day, a great storm swept over the grove. Birds, mice, and other small creatures ran around seeking shelter.

"Oh, Tamarind tree, may we shelter in your canopy?" asked the birds and mice.

"Go away. You cannot stay here. You will ruin my fruits," whispered Tamarind tree.

Shivering with cold, the animals ran to Guava tree, but before the birds and mice could speak, Guava tree whispered, "You cannot stay here." It shook its branches to scare them away.

The animals ran to Tree-with-no-name and asked, "Oh big and mighty tree, may we shelter in your canopy?"

Tree-with-no-name whispered, because all trees whisper, "Come."

The tree stood strong against the storm. It had no name and could not bear fruit but it was glad to help its new little friends.

When the storm passed, Tree-with-no-name whispered goodbye to the birds and field mice. Then a butterfly landed on one of its branches. It was the most beautiful creature the tree had ever seen. The sun shone through its golden wings and the tree realized that this was not a butterfly. The creature transformed into an ethereal being. A Diwata.

"For showing great kindness to all the small creatures of the grove, I will give you a special gift," said the Diwata. "You are a tree of great heart, so you shall bear a wonderful heart-shaped fruit, golden and sweet. You will be known as Mango tree."

As the sun rose high in the sky, the Diwata smiled and disappeared. The tree's branches suddenly felt heavy. Under its canopy hung fragrant, golden fruits. It heard the children come into the grove with their baskets. The tree watched them and felt them climb its trunk.

The tree whispered to them, because all trees whisper, "I am Mango tree."

"The end."

A smile lifted the corners of Mama's mouth. "Read me another."

It hit me then. I had said the same exact words to her when *she* used to read to *me*, before the gambling, before the fire. I turned the page, swallowing the lump in my throat, and read the next story. And the next.

After an hour, Mama placed her hand on my shoulder. "More tea."

I helped her raise her head so she could drink from the cup. It was almost empty. I lifted the edge of the netting and refilled it from the bottle Lola had brought.

"Thank you, anak." Her voice was soft, raspy. "I'm so sorry I disappointed you."

"It's okay, Mama. Just rest. You'll get better, you'll see."

When I moved to turn away, Mama grabbed my wrist and pulled me closer. Her hot breath fanned my cheek. "Promise me, if something happens to me . . ."

"Don't talk that way. You will get well, I know it!"

"Stubborn girl! Listen to me. Please." Mama stared at me; the whites of her eyes had turned yellow. After I nodded, she continued. "If something happens to me, you must ask Mang Rudy to take you to Rosie. She knows how to contact your uncle. She has all the information. Promise me you will do everything you can to leave this place."

I wanted to tell her that I had already tried calling him, but instead I nodded, wiping the tears off my cheeks. She stared at the roof of the darkening grave house until her eyes closed again. Her face felt hot and dry to the touch. A small shallow basin sat by Mama's feet. A rag lay submerged in water and alcohol. I began bathing Mama's face and arms.

"You will get better," I whispered. "You have to."

Chapter Twenty

Mama's fever continued to rage. Lola's lagundi tea and the medicine I bought for her gave her a few hours of relief, but it always returned. So did the pain. The swelling on her hip was bigger and so were the red streaks that cut a path over her skin. It also smelled bad.

She grew weaker and ate less. Twice, I was tempted to ask Mang Rudy to help me take her to a hospital, but I kept hoping that Mama would get better, that all I had to do was wait another day. I did go to Aling Lydia for help, but once again, she wasn't home.

If I had Papa's watch, I would've given it to her as a promise to repay the money she would lend me. Tiger didn't have the right to keep it. The more I thought of it, the more I wanted it back.

The next morning, I noticed that the hollow space between Mama's collarbones and neck looked deeper. Her pain and fever made her tremble as she took another pill. Only two were left now. I'd sold the last of the garlands I made yesterday. All the money I made went to basic needs. I didn't have enough to replenish my supply of everlasting daisies. No garlands, no food, no medicine. I had to do something. As I made breakfast and got ready to wash our clothes, my head filled with schemes on how to get Papa's watch back from Tiger. It all boiled down to a drastic one. Just the thought of it made my knees so weak, I nearly dropped the basin of clothes I was carrying.

"Nora!"

I had just stepped out of the grave house with the laundry balanced on my hip. Aling Lydia and Perla were coming down the alley, each of them carrying a basket.

The jolt of surprise felt like an electrical shock.

Perla gave her mother my message.

But what are they doing here?

I stared at them, my mouth opening and closing, forming words without sound. I set down the basin. Queasiness spread from my stomach to my chest. The bucket we used for a toilet hadn't been emptied. At least I'd remembered to cover it with a piece of cardboard. I watched Aling Lydia and Perla approach and wondered if they would notice the smell. My stomach quivered with embarrassment. I tried to squash it down by smoothing my hair and straightening my clothes.

Aling Lydia nodded to me in greeting. Her round powdered face looked serious. Dark penciled brows arched higher than usual over her eyes. Perla was still in her school uniform. She looked around, her eyes growing larger as she peered into each mausoleum, probably from seeing the television in Mang Rudy's place and the woven cradle suspended from the ceiling in Tess's grave house. Perla tugged at her mother's sleeve, whispering, but her mother waved her away dismissively.

"Nora, I'm so sorry I wasn't home when you came to the house. I was very relieved to hear that your mother is home! Perla told me you said she is very sick. What happened to her?" She gazed at me, her eyes wide with curiosity. It felt like the gossipy sort but I could see how her brow crinkled and how she frowned after saying the word "sick." She seemed truly concerned.

I opened and closed my mouth again, the words starting and then stopping. I wondered if I should tell her the truth.

She waved her hand in the air between us, shaking her head. "Never mind. You can tell me another time if you like. Let me see your mother."

I hesitated. The queasiness in my stomach moved and became a lump in my throat. Shame made my body stiff, and for a minute, I didn't move. Then I pushed it away. I didn't want to feel that way anymore.

"She's inside." Mama and I never had any visitors before.

Normal ones, that is. *Let them see how we live.* I slid the basin of laundry to the side, opened the door to the grave house, and led them in.

Self-consciousness made me take a good look around. The floor had been swept. Papa's picture and the small plastic table were dusted. Even the capiz chimes looked brighter. They tinkled in the soft breeze. Lola must've cleaned while she looked after Mama. I had been too pre-occupied to notice.

Aling Lydia handed Perla her basket. She knelt outside the kulambo covering Mama's sleeping figure. "Lorna? It's me, Lydia." She crawled underneath the netting and grasped the hand Mama held out to her.

I sat on my pink-and-yellow mat, listening to their murmuring voices.

Perla stood at the entrance. She seemed frozen, clutching two baskets to her chest. Her large eyes were fixed on Papa's tomb. After a minute, she shook her head, as if trying to shake an image out of her mind. She looked at me. The corners of her mouth twitched upward.

"So this is where you live?"

It sounded like a fair question. "Yes."

She cast her eyes down, biting her lower lip. There was a mole below her left eye. Funny, I'd never noticed it before.

Perla glanced at her mom. She sighed, her shoulders drooping. She shuffled forward and sat on the mat beside me with her legs folded in front of her and began picking at her nails.

"Isn't it scary? I mean sleeping here with—with—"

"Dead people?"

She glanced up at me, still picking at her nails.

"It isn't the dead people you have to worry about."

"What do you mean?"

"Remember the last day I worked? Some guys broke the lock on our mausoleum gate and stole the money I had been saving and my father's watch. I caught them in the act. If my neighbor, another squatter living up the alley, hadn't come over, those guys would've hurt me." My voice faltered. "Really bad."

"That *is* scarier." Her eyes shifted sideways to look at me, then at the gate. She frowned, her brow wrinkled with concentration. "I hope you replaced that lock. On top of that, you should use a nail. That's what my father did. He drilled a hole into the tile, right in front of the door. At night, we slide a metal rod into it. Even if someone broke the lock they wouldn't be able to get inside."

I nodded, making a mental note to ask Mang Rudy about doing that. We both looked away, too embarrassed to say anything else. It felt awkward sitting together but not speaking, so I leaned over and said, "You know, sometimes I hear scratching sounds at night."

Perla's eyes widened. She turned her head, her eyes scanning the grave house, her ponytail whipping back and forth. "Really? Eww, are there mice here?"

I cupped a hand around my mouth and whispered, "I hear the scratching at night. It sounded close and when

I pressed my ear to the tomb, I realized the sound was coming from *inside*."

"What?!" Perla jerked back, her hand over her mouth.

My lips began to twitch; then I couldn't hold it in, and laughed.

Perla's eyes narrowed. Then she smiled and giggled. "Good one."

She began unpacking the baskets. There were a couple bags of pandesal, some tins of sardines, and mangoes. There were also some packets of medicine. The other basket contained a few old clothes for Mama and me, and a couple of lightweight blankets. She chattered away the whole time, telling me how to open the sardine tins. Maybe I had been wrong about her. Maybe I thought her bossiness meant she was mean, when all along, she was just shy, like me.

Aling Lydia had crawled out of the kulambo and was now walking around the tomb to where Perla and I sat.

"Nora, your mother needs to go to the hospital. You have to take her as soon as you can. I wish I could lend you money for this but I don't have very much cash right now, what with my ovens in the bakery breaking down one after the other." She shook her fist into the air as if the gods of luck were standing before her. "Your mother said something about a brother in Davao. You must call him. Come to the bakery later on."

"One of my neighbors has a cell phone. I tried calling my uncle, but I haven't been able to reach him. I will try again soon." I stood, holding my hands behind me to keep from fidgeting.

"Good. I'd offer my cell phone but it's almost out of power. You are also welcome to use our phone in the bakery." She signaled her daughter to stand. "Let's go, anak. You have homework to do."

Perla made a face. "Bye, Nora. I hope you hear from your uncle soon." She followed her mother out of the grave house.

I watched them go, and then stared at the supplies they had brought. I wouldn't have to worry about food or medicine for a few days. The relief I felt was short-lived. Dread took its place, reminding me that I had to get Papa's watch back, in case Tito Danny couldn't come.

Aling Lydia's words weighed heavy on my mind. I checked on Mama. She was sleeping, but she looked pale, shrunken on the mat. *I will not let her die.* With renewed determination, I left, closing the grave house door gently, and picked up my basin of laundry.

There was a small cement area behind the grave house where Mama and I did the wash and the dishes. We took our baths there too. A large plastic water bucket sat by the wall. Yesterday, the container was nearly empty, but not anymore. The battered basin next to it was also full of water. Jojo had probably come by early this morning, because there were no mosquito larvae wriggling around below the surface of the water. How did he know I was doing the wash today? A bar of laundry soap sat next to the basin.

Even the block of wood I used as a bench was already in place.

Someone was whistling. Jojo's smiling face appeared around the side of the grave house carrying a pile of clothes. "*Hoy!* What are you doing here?"

"I live here?" He seemed surprised to see me. What was he up to this time?

"No, I meant, are you about to do your wash?" Jojo asked.

"Hmmm . . . yeah, along with yours, since you have it already."

"Actually, I came over to help you. I figured I'd do my own stuff since you had to take care of your mother."

"Oh. Well, that's nice of you. Salamat." I set my basin of clothes next to the one filled with water.

He nodded toward it. "That looks big enough for both of us to use. That is, if you don't mind."

"I don't mind." While I balanced myself on my make-shift bench, Jojo simply squatted. We both plunged our hands in the water at the same time.

"How's your mother doing?" asked Jojo. *Scrub, scrub, scrub.*

"She gets worse every day." *Scrub, scrub, scrub.*

"Does she need more lagundi tea?" *Scrub, scrub, wring.*

"I guess she could use some more. Aling Lydia and Perla brought some food and medicine but we will run out sooner or later. She's going to need that and more." *Scrub, wring, wring.*

"More penicillin?" *Wring, wring, plop.*

"That and a doctor's visit. Or better, a trip to a hospital. But I would need to pay for her medicines and the taxi ride to get her there. I tried calling my uncle but I haven't been able to reach him. I'll have to come up with some money fast. Either today or tomorrow." Should I tell him my plan? Or was it better to keep it to myself?

"So what are you going to do?" He looked at me with wide-eyed concern. Flecks of foam stuck to his cheeks and eyebrows. "Are you thinking about speaking to Aling Lydia? Maybe she can lend you the money."

"I did talk to her. She didn't have any cash for me to borrow. Her bakery ovens needed repair. Besides, I don't have anything to give as a guarantee that I'd pay her back. Anyway, I came up with another plan."

After finally wringing out the shirt he was washing, he paused, resting his dripping hands on his knees. "What is it?"

There was no turning back now. "You know that Tiger stole my father's watch, right?"

"Uh-huh," he said with his mouth hanging slightly open, waiting for me to continue.

"Well . . . I want to steal it back. He's not going to be at his grave house this afternoon and his friends follow him like a pack of hungry stray dogs. It would be easy. I could sneak in when he's not there, grab the watch, and run for it. And you could be my lookout." The words slipped off my tongue like melted ice cream. Had I really asked him to be my eyes? It made sense after I had said it. I would feel better about doing this if Jojo was with me.

I wanted to tell him that Tiger had a new watch and that he probably wouldn't miss my father's old one, but I didn't.

He had a queer expression on his face, as if I had just told him I was the Virgin Mary.

"What?"

A smile tugged at the corners of his wide mouth. He suddenly burst out laughing. It wasn't the usual "ha ha ha" laugh. It sounded loud and harsh. "You can't be serious!" he said between spasms of laughter that erupted every time he looked at me.

My cheeks tingled with heat. "I *am* serious. I could take it to a pawn shop, and . . ."

"No way! You're crazy to want to go near his hideout again. Stay away. Your father's watch is gone. Forget about it." He grabbed a duster from his pile and slammed it into the soapy water, still chuckling.

How could he laugh at me? Of course he would think my plan was crazy, but what Mama was going through wasn't. He could think whatever he wanted.

We finished our wash with Jojo telling me how he collected recyclables, and about some of the colors he used when he painted tombs, like pink, sky blue, and pale green. He said it made part of the cemetery look like a rainbow. I kept my lips pressed together the whole time, still too annoyed to speak.

I hung the clothes to dry while he emptied the basins.

My irritation strengthened my resolve to do what needed to be done. I was determined to go through with my plan, with or without him. Not talking to him was a good way of keeping things to myself. Also, I didn't want to argue with him.

"I'm sorry I laughed at you." Jojo tapped me on the shoulder. "Come on, talk to me again. You have to admit that your plan is crazy, right? And dangerous?"

"Yeah. I know." The line vibrated as I snapped the wet clothes open before hanging them.

"Look, I know the watch was important to you and I know how much you think you need it, but having anything to do with Tiger can only mean trouble. Lola and I can help you find the money for your mother; it might take a few days but we'll find it." Jojo's eyes were wide with pleading, his brows furrowed. "Promise me you won't try to steal the watch? I don't want you to get hurt."

I could feel my resolve cracking but my desperation was stronger. We didn't have a few days. My stomach growled. Mama was so ill. Hunger and sickness made people want to do stupid things.

There was no way I could make that promise but I couldn't tell him that. So I shrugged and waved goodbye when it was time for him to leave for work.

Back inside the grave house, Mama continued to sleep. She lay so still, I had to hold my hand in front of her mouth to feel her hot, shallow breath. I made sure a covered glass of water was within her reach, along with some of the medicine. It helped her sleep but only for a short period of time. The fever was now constant. She needed something stronger. She needed to see a doctor. The kulambo covered her completely, protecting her from the flies that sickness attracted like bees to flowers. With the sheet drawn across the bars against prying eyes, I stepped out into the alley.

It was time.

Chapter Twenty-one

THE HIDDEN POCKET ON MY WAISTBAND WAS EMPTY except for the balisong. The hard shape of it pressed against my stomach, quieting the butterflies that fluttered there.

My first thought was to follow the main road into the Chinese cemetery. I decided against it. That would be like walking into a cage of angry monkeys, as Jojo liked to say. It would be better to use the shortcut we'd taken a few days ago.

I found the gate and crawled through it before I could talk myself into turning back. My heart thudded in my chest like a fist punching a wall.

The electrical box and the caged yard were just as I had last seen them. The gap Jojo had made at the bottom of the fence was still there. Without hesitation, I wriggled through to the other side, with the grave houses of the rich dead looming over me.

I slipped the balisong out of my pocket. I held it the way Jojo taught me, with my thumb resting near the release clip. The way to Tiger's hideout was deserted. I stayed close to the buildings so I could hide at a moment's notice. It was the hottest part of the day, just two hours past noon. I hoped I would find Tiger's grave house as empty as the streets.

There was no sound except for the distant melody of a funeral march and the soft slap of my slippers against my heels. I ducked behind the low wall of the grave house next to the one Tiger lived in. The two-story building of Mr. Santiago's family crypt looked empty.

I tiptoed to the front gate of the grave house and listened for any sound of movement or conversation. Nothing. My hand was on the gate, ready to pull it open, when I heard footsteps and voices coming from the other side of the building. I jumped behind the low wall just as two men emerged from around the corner.

They were the very same thugs who had been with Tiger when he ransacked my place. It was the bowlegged one and the one that looked like a matchstick. They sat on the stoop and lit cigarettes. How was I supposed to get in there now?

"What a great place the boss has upstairs. The whole building has electricity!"

"Yeah, he's really tight with that Mr. Santiago. I heard he gets to work at the grocery store soon."

"Night security or something, right? Ha! Security. What a joke."

"Yeah? Well, if he's gonna give up this place, I'll take over as caretaker. Hey, is he home? Maybe we can check out what he's got upstairs." *Smack.* "Aray! What was that for?"

"Hunger is making you stupid. Come on, let's go get a snack."

"Tiger told us to wait for him here. We're supposed to be watching the place, remember?"

"Sige na, we'll be quick. There's a woman a few streets over who makes great banana-que."

Their voices faded. As soon as they turned the corner at the end of the street, I bolted out of my hiding place. I was inside Tiger's grave house in just a few seconds. I probably had only a few minutes to search and then get out.

The first floor of the grave house had a single tomb, made with marble so shiny I could see myself on its polished surface. It dominated the middle of the room. Where were the stairs to the second floor? I looked all around me, my throat tightening with panic.

There they were, located in the corner, painted the same color as the back wall. Metal stairs twisted up and around a pole, into the floor above. They blended in so well I almost didn't see them.

The steps clanged as I ran up. I found a small landing and a screen door at the top. It had no handle, just a keyhole. I grabbed the frame and pulled. It wouldn't budge. I stared at the room beyond. There were no tombs on the upper level of this grave house. The room looked like a small apartment. It had a worn old couch set against one wall. A TV sat on a crate in front of it. Against another wall stood a bed with a rusty metal frame and a thin mattress covered with a bright bedsheet. Next to it was a table full of small knotted bags, a black metal box, and other odds and ends like old containers and food wrappers.

Disappointed, I turned to leave, when something shiny caught my eye. A black comb lay on the edge of the table, and next to it, partially covered by a balled-up paper food wrapper, was the silver wristband of Papa's watch. I shook the locked gate in frustration. I needed to open it, but how?

I stared at the keyhole. It looked rusty with age. Would the balisong fit? I snapped the butterfly knife open and looked closely at the blade. It looked about the right size. I gently eased the thin blade into the slit and wriggled it around. Sweat trickled down my face as I moved the blade up and down, then side to side.

Voices drifted up to me from the street. I gasped, my heart galloping in my chest. A high-pitched whine escaped from my throat the closer the voices got to the grave house. The door lock clicked just as the men stepped inside. The slap of their rubber slippers echoed through the structure. The aroma of fried bananas wafted into the air. My hand clutched at my stomach. *Please don't growl.* I stood frozen on the landing, my back pressed against the screen door. I could see their shadows moving against the wall below.

"Did we leave the gate open? Tiger would kill us if he found out," said one man.

"What difference would it make? The second floor is locked up," said the other.

The slapping sound of slippers came closer to the stairs. My hands tightened around the balisong. My breathing quickened as my panic grew. I held the knife out in front of me.

"Come on, let's sit outside. It's hot in here." Their footsteps moved away from the stairs.

After making sure they were outside, I turned once again to the door and pulled on the frame. It was still locked. The mechanism had probably snapped back into place when I pulled the knife out. I moaned and started to pick the lock again when I heard shouting coming from the street. If that was Tiger coming back, then I'd better get out of here. I crept down the stairs and hid behind the space between the back wall and the tomb. I chanced a peek to see if the coast was clear. It wasn't.

A policeman was standing right outside the grave house. He stopped the two men before they could find a place to sit.

"There will be a funeral coming through. You guys have to leave," said the policeman, pointing down the street.

"But we work here," said one of them. "Our boss won't pay us if he finds out we left. We're supposed to be watching this place."

"Sure you are. You can come back after the funeral passes," said the policeman, talking exaggeratedly slow.

"Just so you know, there will be another one coming through this area tomorrow. There will be TV people present for that one, so you can't be here. We can't have you squatters hanging around. Now move!" He waved a black baton at them, pointing away from the coming funeral.

"No problem, boss. We'll just hang out behind the building."

The sound of their footsteps and complaints faded, only to be replaced by the scratchy sound of funerary music. A white hearse drove slowly by. Inside was a coffin draped in flowers. There were people walking alongside the car but most of the mourners walked behind it. They carried a colorful array of umbrellas to shield them from the sun. A band of musicians followed, playing a repeating stream of funerary music.

Should I go upstairs and try again? The funeral procession would soon pass the grave house and those thugs would be back. I would have to return tomorrow when the next funeral procession came this way.

After the last car passed, I ran out of the grave house as fast as I could to the shortcut in the outer wall. I crawled under the fence of the utility shed, relieved that I'd made it out safely. But I had been so close. So close to having Papa's watch in my hand again. So close to getting help for Mama.

With the balisong safely tucked back into my pocket, I passed through the little gate and found Jojo standing on the other side. And he was *mad*.

Chapter Twenty-two

Jojo stood there and scowled at me. It looked like he had just returned from the market. He carried a basket containing two small fish, bananas, and some vegetables. I waited for him to say something and when he didn't, I tried to walk past him.

He stepped in front of me and said, "Where did you just come from? No, let me guess. You went to confront Tiger and asked him to let you have your father's watch back." He continued to scowl at me while he waited for my answer.

"And what if I did?" If he wanted a fight, he was going to get one. I wasn't about to let anyone stand between me and what I needed to do for my mother.

"Oh you did, huh? Then you are . . ."

"What? What am I? I'm just a stupid girl who cares if her mother lives or dies."

"But you can't just talk to Tiger like he's some ordinary guy. He's dangerous."

"You want to know what I did? I tried to sneak into his place. If Tiger's friends hadn't shown up, I would've had the watch in my hands right now." This time I pushed past him, hoping he didn't see the tremble in my lower lip. I wasn't going to cry. But before I broke into a run, he grabbed my arm and spun me around to face him.

"You really don't care what happens to you, do you?" Jojo asked. His scowl melted in front of my eyes. Now, he just looked defeated.

"Of course I do. I'm alone and scared. But I will not sit around and watch my mother die."

"But you're not alone. I'm here to help you. Look, I just got paid and I'm bringing some food to your grave house. All your mother needs is fresh food. Lola's gonna make a soup with the fish and vegetables. The bananas are the small ones your mother likes." He swung the basket in front of me to show me how fresh the fish were, their eyes clear and not bloodshot. Then he led me to the sidewalk. "Do you really think your mother is dying?"

I nodded. We headed back toward the main cemetery gate, both of us lost in thought. Jojo's face was somber, his brows drawn together in concentration. Frustrated, he punched the air and said, "There has to be a way to find enough money. Another, safer way."

"There are other ways, Jojo. But they all take time. My mother is running *out* of time." The memory of Mama's feverish skin flashed through my mind and made me more impatient for the next day.

"Hey, how about this?" He jogged over to an electric pole tacked with advertisements, old and new. Jojo grabbed a bright yellow flyer and handed it to me. "I saw this earlier. I know what you're going to say but just hear me out. This could be about a job. Maybe you can ask the nuns for help. They do this kind of charity, don't they?"

I looked down at the flyer in his hands.

"This isn't about a job, Jojo. It's about a scholarship program." It was the same one Kuya Efren had told me about. I folded the paper and tucked it into my shorts pocket, remembering the reviewer and application forms I already had.

"Well, why not just go and ask if they can help? I've seen them visit sick people in the cemetery before."

I shook my head. "I can't take that chance. No. I'm sticking to my plan and taking back what belongs to Mama and me. By this time tomorrow, I'll be able to take her to the hospital."

Jojo opened his mouth to say something. I interrupted him and said, "I know, I know, it's dangerous. But if I got through it today, I'm sure I'll get through it tomorrow."

His face was still clouded with anger. I wasn't about to back down. "Listen. There is going to be a big funeral tomorrow of some important person passing right by Tiger's grave house. No one will be there. We could do this together. One of us can stand guard while the other gets the watch."

"Hey, wait a minute. What is this *we* business? I'm not going to sneak into Tiger's place and neither should you. It would be suicide, plain and simple," said Jojo, his face so close to mine that I could feel the heat of his breath.

"But it wouldn't be, because no one will be there. Don't you see? It's the perfect chance."

"No."

"But . . ."

"I said, *no*. You were lucky to get out of there alive today, because you can be sure that if you had been caught, you would wish you had listened to me." He turned and walked away, wiping furiously at his eyes.

What could I say? He was right. But what if I succeeded? I had to try, for Mama's sake. I could see now that if I went through with it, I would hurt Jojo. I caught up to him but he refused to look at me.

Then he stopped and faced me, his eyes still shiny with tears. He didn't look angry anymore. "Nora, please, don't go back to Tiger's place. Wait for me tomorrow, and if you still want to go, then I'll go with you. But hopefully you'll change your mind about it by then, because I have a plan."

"What do you mean?"

"Please, Nora, please? Say you'll wait for me before you go? I promise I'll be at your place early. I promise!"

"What are you thinking of doing?"

"Please, just promise."

"Okay, I promise. But you have to tell me what you're planning to do."

"I'll tell you everything tomorrow. I'll be there early. Come on, let's get this basket to Lola before she decides to boil her slipper for soup."

We continued walking in silence. As we passed Ibarra's bakery, I glanced inside, searching for Aling Lydia. She was there and so was Perla. For just a moment, the urge to run over to the bakery and beg for money overwhelmed me, but I knew she wouldn't be able to help me. Besides, Aling Lydia was busy talking to a nun with an armful of yellow paper. They both turned to look my way. I ducked my head down and quickened my pace.

When we reached the cemetery gate, the policeman I saw earlier was busy directing the line of cars from another funeral into the flow of traffic.

"Jojo, go on ahead. I have to ask that policeman something."

I stepped into the street and glanced back to make sure he heard me. Jojo stood where I left him, staring at me with one eyebrow raised. I waved him away and smiled to reassure him that everything was fine and that I wasn't up to anything crazy. He finally turned with a shake of his head and walked into the throng of visitors exiting the cemetery.

"Excuse me, sir." The policeman didn't hear me. I repeated myself, then tapped him on the arm. He turned his frowning brown face in my direction. His eyes were like slits. His bushy brows were drawn together; sweat dripped at his temples. The skin on his cheeks was rough with acne scars, and the corners of his wide mouth were turned down in distaste.

"What do you want? Can't you see I'm busy here?" asked the policeman. He continued to wave cars out of the cemetery gate with one hand while holding the other up to keep street traffic in the other direction stopped.

"Sir, will there be a funeral like this one tomorrow?" It seemed like a stupid question to ask, since this was a cemetery, and there were always funerals going on for the rich and poor alike.

"Today a banker from Makati; tomorrow, a councilman from Sampaloc," mumbled the policeman as he continued directing traffic.

"Sir, will it be at the same time as today's?" I winced when he scowled at me again. Then he turned away and didn't even bother to answer my question.

How rude! Well, at least he'd confirmed that there would be a funeral tomorrow. Maybe if I waited at the gate early enough, I'd know when it started, and could be through the shortcut to Tiger's place before the procession actually got there. Hopefully Jojo would keep his promise and be at my grave house early. It occurred to me that he might be planning to stop me from going to Tiger's place tomorrow. But I was sure that once he saw how sick Mama was, he would agree to go with me.

The sky had turned from blue to gray. Clouds covered the sky like a blanket. It was time to go home. My stomach grumbled. I walked through the main gate, against the flow of visitors and street vendors leaving the cemetery. Once I got free of the crowd, I jogged home, hoping to entice Mama's appetite with the prospect of soup from Lola.

When I finally turned the corner into my alley, Aling Nena came running up to meet me. She was a thin woman, with hair cut so short at the back that you could see her scalp peeking through. Her eyes were small and so close together she looked almost cross-eyed. They were wide open now, her brows furrowed with worry. "Thank goodness you're back! Where have you been? Your mother went looking for you. I tried to stop her and get her to lie down but she wouldn't listen. She kept saying 'wait' and 'don't leave me.' She didn't even want me to walk with her. So I had little Ernie follow her. Quick. They can't be far."

Aling Nena continued to babble apologetically while my mind whirled. Why would Mama come looking for me? Did she figure out that the watch was missing?

The sky darkened to a steel gray. The first drops of rain hit the top of my head with surprising coolness. I had to find Mama fast.

Chapter Twenty-three

I FOUND THEM BY THE SIDE OF THE ROAD NOT FAR from our alley. Ernie tried to help Mama stand. But she kept losing her balance. According to Ernie, she had collapsed and hit her forehead on a nearby tomb. She had a horrible bump on her head and a cut that dripped blood in the pouring rain.

With Ernie's help, I got Mama on her feet. She leaned her full weight on me as we walked home, my arm clasped around her waist. By the time we reached the grave house, the rain had plastered our hair to our skulls and was dripping from our clothes. I thanked little Ernie and sent him home.

Mama moaned when I set her down on the mat. She grabbed my arm and said, "Anak. I saw your papa."

"Shhhh. It was a dream, Mama. Now calm down and rest. You shouldn't have gone out in the rain like that."

She stared at me with eyes that were sunken and hot with fever. "No, I wasn't dreaming. I really saw your papa, Nora. He stood right in front of me. He touched my face. Then he smiled at me and asked me what time it was. He asked me that three times."

The hairs all over my body stood on end. It made me shiver even though the air was warm and humid from the rain. "What do you think Papa was trying to tell you?"

"I don't know." Her eyes were shiny with tears. "He said that I had to find you. Then he turned to leave. I didn't want him to go, so I followed him." Mama's voice trailed off into a whisper, her eyes focused on some distant memory.

My own eyes burned and my vision blurred. Mama was deteriorating fast. I pushed the thought away, cleared my throat, and said, "Mama, please. Rest. Everything will be fine tomorrow, you'll see. Just hang on."

It was so hard to be brave when all I wanted to do was cry.

It wasn't until we both changed into dry clothes that I noticed two small iron pots in the corner of the grave house. One contained the fish-and-vegetable soup Jojo had promised, and the other some boiled rice. "Mama, look! Jojo left us something hot for dinner." She didn't answer and continued to stare at nothing. I fed Mama as much as she could eat, right out of the pots. I ate when she was done, saving the rest for breakfast.

I placed the pots in a basin of water, to prevent ants from getting to the food. Beside it stood my sweet potato plant, its leaves and stems now completely brown. I moved the pot outside. Maybe the rain would revive it. The soil the plant grew in would be soaked by morning. I wished it would survive. It seemed pretty hopeless though. Once the door was locked, I hung up the kulambo over Mama. Then I crawled underneath it and stretched out next to her sleeping form.

My muscles and bones ached, but I couldn't sleep. The rain tapped on the roof of the grave house, making it hard to hear Mama's breathing. It was coming down harder now.

Mama had shown me how to plant sweet potatoes when we first moved to the cemetery using a few leaves from Lola Fely's garden. Jojo and I had found a large bucket, made a couple of drain holes on the bottom, and filled it with dirt. Together, we'd carried it back to Mama.

She'd held up a stem with heart-shaped leaves and pointed to a small green bump near the bottom. "Do you see this? When you bury this in the dirt, it will grow into roots. Then in about six weeks, we will have sweet potatoes for roasting!"

We had harvested four of them, each one the size of a banana. We gave two to Lola and Jojo and one to our neighbor Tina, who had been pregnant at the time. Mama had sliced off a piece of the remaining one, then roasted the rest of it in a small oven she made with rocks. While it cooked, she showed me a bump or "eye" she'd cut off the sweet potato, then buried it in the dirt. We repeated this process every six or eight weeks.

Now there would be none. The thought made my chest ache. I watched Mama breathe until my eyes grew so heavy that when I blinked, I didn't open them again until morning.

Mama was still asleep when I left for the gate. I waited for Jojo as long as I could. What had happened to him? He'd begged me to wait and then he didn't show up. Well, he couldn't say that I didn't give him a chance.

The streets were still wet from the previous night's rain. Black muddy spots covered my calves and my shorts. The cemetery gate was crowded with the usual visitors and vendors. After checking for approaching funeral processions, I sat in a shady spot by the road. I rested my head against the cool cement of a tomb. Hopefully the wait wouldn't be too long.

Time crawled by as the sun rose to its highest point in the sky. My eyelids grew heavy. I closed my eyes, telling myself I was just resting them, but I drifted off anyway.

I dreamed about Jojo. In the dream, he was asking me a question, but I didn't understand him. All I could hear was a sad melody that played over and over again. It sounded like—funeral music.

My eyes flew open, expecting to see a procession passing by, but instead I was looking at a little girl with large brown eyes and a sharp chin. She was crouched in front of me, wearing faded denim shorts and a pink T-shirt that looked too big for her small body.

"Hey, you're awake. You better get out of here or the police will get you. Got any spare change?" asked the little girl. She was eyeing my pocket to see if I had anything in there.

"Uh, no. I don't." The street was empty except for the usual foot traffic. The faint strains of a funeral march caught my ear. "Hey, did a funeral pass by here a little while ago?"

The little girl's face brightened. "Oh, yes! A big one with lots of cars. I walked up to one and tapped on the window and a woman inside gave me five pesos. I wanted to try the next car but the policeman saw me and shooed me away. I ran over here to watch the rest of the cars go by. That's how I found you."

"Which way did it go?"

The girl pointed toward the Chinese cemetery. With a hasty thank-you, I ran to the end of the street and rounded the corner. There it was!

The funeral procession was huge. At the head of the line were a couple of policemen on motorcycles. The car that followed carried a coffin covered with wreaths of red and white flowers. There were mourners following it on foot, with more riding in cars behind them. Running alongside the vehicles were squatter children waving and knocking on the windows, begging for money. I caught up to them, trying to blend in.

When it reached Tiger's grave house, I hid behind one of the lion statues by the door. The mausoleum looked deserted. Once the funeral procession turned the corner, I went inside.

I climbed the metal stairs as quietly as I could, ready to bolt back down in case Tiger was there. He wasn't. The door at the top was locked just as before. I snapped open the balisong and inserted the tip into the keyhole. Sweat dripped down my forehead and into my eyes. My hands shook so much, the knife slipped out several times.

After taking a deep breath, I inserted the balisong again, moving it slowly until I felt it catch on something inside the lock. With a twist, it snapped, and the door swung open.

I headed straight for the table, where Papa's watch lay among the debris of food wrappings and Tiger's personal items. Next to it was an envelope with Mama's name scrawled across the front. I looked inside and saw a stack of purple one-hundred-peso bills. Tiger must've switched the envelopes just before the taxi was supposed to take Mama home. I rolled the bundle up and stuffed it into my pocket. I slipped Papa's watch onto my wrist, pressing my lips to it.

I skipped to the door. Mama was going to see the doctor as soon as I got home.

With the balisong still in my hand, I closed the door with a *clank* and froze. The crunchy sound of tires on cement echoed through the grave house. Then I heard the *click* and *thud* of car doors opening and closing, along with the muffled sound of voices. My heart thumped against my ribs and my hands shook so much that the balisong slipped out of my sweaty hands. It clattered down the metal staircase and landed on the cement floor, spinning out of sight. I held my breath and waited for someone to rush into the grave house and find me. But no one came.

Maybe those people were visiting another grave house. *Please let it be so.* Blood pounded in my ears as I crept down the stairs and hid behind the tomb. I could see the car from where I was hiding. Three guys were leaning against it, smoking cigarettes.

No. One of them was the skinny man I saw yesterday.

"I wish Tiger would hurry up and get here." The thug flicked his cigarette to drop the ash on the ground. He was a heavy-looking fellow with a large brown face and a short, spiky haircut.

"Yeah, well, he better get here soon. The boss doesn't like to be kept waiting," said the skinny one.

How was I going to get out of here? I fought down the panic clenching my throat like a vise. *Stay. Calm. Think!* If I could get to the door without any of them noticing me, then I could make a run for it. I'd have a better chance if

I had the balisong pointed at them. They wouldn't mess with someone with a knife, right? I looked around. Where was it?

The balisong lay against the wall, right next to the gate. Could I get to it without being seen? I'd have to be very quiet. I stepped out of my slippers. With bare feet, I padded across the floor.

I was halfway to the gate when I heard the voice that turned my blood to ice and my courage to ashes.

Chapter Twenty-four

"WHERE'S THE KID?" ASKED TIGER. I CLAMPED MY hand over my mouth to keep from screaming.

"In the backseat, boss," said another voice.

"Did anyone see you? Did he put up much of a fight?" asked Tiger.

"Nope. We taped him up real good and got him in the car before the funeral came around. Why do you want him, boss?" said one of the men.

"The stupid kid thought I wasn't home last night and tried to sneak in. He ran before I could get to him."

"Why don't we just beat him up? Teach him a lesson?"

"I thought of that but I got a better idea. I'll turn him over to Mr. Santiago and tell him the brat tried to steal one of the porcelain flower vases his wife bought recently for the mausoleum. He'll send the kid to prison for that. The police will believe him over the kid. Getting his butt kicked will be nothing compared to rotting in jail. Wait here while I get my keys."

A kid tried to sneak into Tiger's grave house?

My mind raced. Jojo had said he had a plan. Then he didn't show up this morning.

No. It can't be . . .

Tiger came into view and opened the gate of the grave house. I pulled myself back into my hiding place. I made myself as small as possible so he wouldn't see me. The sound of rushing blood filled my ears. *Please don't see me, please don't see me.*

Tiger ran up the stairs, unlocked his door, and went into his room. He hadn't caught sight of me but he could when he came back down. There had to be another place to hide, but there wasn't. I crouched low as he climbed down the steps and headed out the door. He was too busy sorting through a set of keys to notice me.

It was a good thing Tiger hadn't seen the balisong either. I had to try to get it now or risk being caught without a way to defend myself.

After making sure Tiger was outside, I tiptoed over and snatched up the butterfly knife. With my body pressed against the wall, I peered out the gate. I couldn't see the kid inside the car.

Tiger had his back to me, and his gang stood beside him

facing the car. It would be risky, but if I could sneak out, I could run and hide somewhere outside before they even noticed me. I just had to wait for the right moment to step out.

Tiger handed a set of keys to one of the guys and said, "This opens the back door to the boss's building. Make your way south on Bonifacio Avenue. Remember, Santiago's Grocery is across the street from the Chinese General Hospital. Park at the back of the building and get the kid in there quickly. I'll meet you there."

Something thudded against the inside of the car door, as if someone was trying to kick it open. Tiger looked into the vehicle and rapped on the window.

"You better stop that or I'll beat you myself for ruining my boss's car," shouted Tiger. He pounded the door with his fist. "It serves you right for trying to break into my room last night."

I guess I wasn't the only one trying to steal from Tiger. The thought made me cringe, remembering what Jojo told me yesterday. *Please don't let it be Jojo.* What were they going to do to that boy? I could find someone to help him but I had to escape first. I took a deep breath and inched out of the gate while Tiger and his gang hurled more abuse at the captive inside the car. "I'm warning you, stop kicking the door or we'll have to tie you up like a pig!" cried one of the men. The thumping continued.

My feet had barely touched the bottom step when Tiger pulled open the back door of the car and said, "Hey, someone grab those feet. Get in. We can't waste any more time. The boss is waiting, so let's get him there as soon as possible."

A familiar head of spiky hair came into view. The boy's face was bruised, his eyes swollen. A strip of cloth had been tied tight between his teeth.

Jojo.

A gasp flew out of my mouth the moment I recognized his battered face.

They all spun around to look at me. Tiger sneered and said, "Well, what's this? And what are you doing coming out of my grave house?" His eyes narrowed at the balisong clutched in my hand. Without taking his eyes from me, he signaled to one of his guys and said, "Go on ahead. You have the keys. We mustn't keep Mr. Santiago waiting."

His gang hesitated, then got into the car and drove away. Tiger stared at me, waiting to see what I would do. I started to move, inching away sideways. He still watched but said nothing. Was he going to let me leave? I breathed in short, terrified gasps. I glanced to my left and saw that I had my chance. I had a clear path to the street.

I bolted. But Tiger was quick. He reached out, grabbed my hair, and pulled me backward. I lost my balance and fell, dropping the balisong as I landed on the edge of the stairs. I scrambled for the blade but Tiger got to it first. He flicked the knife closed, and then flicked it open. Closed. Open. Closed.

Open.

"Where did a worthless squatter like you get a knife like

this?" Tiger stood over me as he ran his finger down the side of the blade.

"Give it back."

"Not so fast," said Tiger. He snapped the balisong closed. "Whoever gave it to you was wise. A young girl needs to protect herself in a place like this. What are you doing here?"

His eyes caught the flash of silver on my wrist before I could hide it behind my back. He grabbed my arm. "Why, you little thief."

"You're the thief! You took this watch from me and you stole my mother's money. Hayop ka!" I said through gritted teeth. He continued to stare at me, chuckling. Before I could stop myself, I spat into his face.

Tiger wiped away the spittle with his free hand. He began to laugh. "What should I do with you?"

He pulled me up and dragged me back into the grave house. I bit the hand that held my arm. He shrieked, then grabbed a handful of my hair.

"Don't make me cut your face!" shouted Tiger. He tried to flick open the balisong while I twisted in his grip. Frustrated, he threw the knife to the floor and bent to swing me over his shoulder so he could carry me up the stairs.

I brought my knee up hard against his face. He reared back screaming, covering his nose with his hands, cursing at me the whole time. I stumbled out the door and scooped up the balisong.

I ran. Panic gave my feet wings. I could hear Tiger

shouting behind me. My feet were numbed to the small rocks and bits of glass I stepped on. They were cutting the bottoms of my feet to ribbons. My chest was tight with the need to stop and take a breath, but I knew that if I stopped, I would die.

All I could think about was finding a place to hide. I found myself in the oldest and emptiest part of the cemetery. I raced through a narrow lane between rows of tombs built so close together, I was sure I'd find somewhere to lie low.

With a quick glance, I realized that Tiger had stopped chasing me. I stopped, breathing hard, my hand pressed against the pain in my side. My panic faded and along with it, the strength in my legs. I dropped to the ground, my whole body shaking with a mixture of relief and misery. I folded the butterfly knife and tucked it into my pocket.

Jojo. I had to find him. But how?

I looked around to figure out which direction my grave house would be in. I'd go home, check on Mama, and then go and find Mang Rudy. Yes, he would know what to do. I stood, my feet burning with pain. I wished I had my slippers, but I'd left them at Tiger's grave house.

Something moved. My head snapped around to look. Nothing. My heart banged in my chest. Nobody was around. It could be a stray dog picking through the trash scattered all over the ground. I took a step forward. Out of the corner of my eye, I gasped and stared, barely breathing, at a grassy spot between two tombs. Could it be Tiger?

A cat leaped out from behind a pile of discarded human bones, making me jump. A sigh escaped from my trembling lips. Tiger had probably given up the chase by now. At least, I hoped so. I had to get to somewhere safe, just in case.

I limped along as fast as my burning feet would allow me, picking my way through a trash heap between an empty crypt and a crumbling wall of apartment tombs. It made me sad to see the bones of people long forgotten, mixed in with the trash.

I heard a snap behind me. It must be the cat. I turned to shoo it away and froze. My breath caught in my throat. Tiger's blood-streaked face loomed over me. I screamed, took a step backward and fell, the back of my head hitting something hard. For a moment, the world was filled with pain.

Then darkness.

Chapter Twenty-five

HAD I DIED? I SAW NOTHING BUT BLACK. NO, I WASN'T dead, but I almost wished I was.

The bump on my head throbbed. I wanted to scream for help, but who would hear me? My eyes felt gritty, my scratched cheeks stung. Probably from being shoved head-first into this suffocating box.

I was inside an empty tomb. My hands were tied behind me and my legs were bound together at the ankles. Pin-pricks of light came through gaps between the rocks Tiger had used to seal up the opening below my feet. I knew he'd pushed me far into the crypt because I couldn't touch the pile of stones, even when I stretched my toes.

How was I going to get out of here? A scream tore

through my throat. This was not the end for me; it couldn't be. Tiger hadn't given up. It was stupid of me to think he would. I should've kept running. Tears seeped from my eyes and ran over my cheeks, which were already tight with dried mucus and dirt. Stupid, stupid girl!

And what had Jojo been thinking? He could've gone with me so that we could protect each other, but no, he had to be a hero. I'd told him that the passing funeral procession would be the best time to get into Tiger's grave house, but he hadn't listened. I should've known he'd try a stunt like that.

I remembered the day he'd showed me his balisong. *I'm not losing another friend to that dog.* If only I'd paid more attention to what he was hinting at, to what he was planning to do, then I could've have stopped him from trying to steal Papa's watch back. I deserved to die for being so selfish. But wasn't it more selfish to just lie here and give up?

My hand brushed something round, papery. I grasped it between my fingers, feeling the points of dry flower petals prick my skin. *Everlasting.* Even in this dark hole, it was still intact, still whole.

A sudden calm came over me. It was as if a string tied around my heart was suddenly cut away. I was not going to give up. I would find a way to get out of this tomb. I ignored the twinge of panic still threatening to overtake me. It was time to get my bearings. The tomb had a sweet, sickly odor that made me want to gag, but I had to breathe. I rolled onto my stomach with my cheek resting on the dirt-covered stone. By shifting my arms back and forth, I tried to pull my hands out of their bindings. But they were tied too tight. I couldn't reach into my pocket for my balisong. A tingling began at the tips of my fingers and spread through my hands.

An insect crawled up my leg. I kicked and thrashed until I couldn't feel it anymore. Blood pounded in my ears as my breath steadied. I rocked my body until I was lying on my side. My hand brushed something hard. A stick. I let go of the daisy and picked it up. Maybe I could use it to cut the strips of cloth tied around my wrists. It was rounded and smooth like a tube, jagged at one end. Was it a piece of wood from an old coffin? I passed the object between my fingers. The other end of it had a wider, knobby shape, and it was hollow in the center.

It was a human bone.

My mind rebelled at the thought of using it as a tool but it was better than nothing. I felt for its rounded end and pushed it against the wall of the tomb behind me. With the jagged edge pointed toward me, I carefully placed the cloth binding on it and pushed down. The bone slipped off the wall. I repositioned it again and again but it would not stay in place. I began to cry.

Don't give up. Don't stop.

I needed to try something different. With the bone in my hand once again, I positioned the round end of it on the lower part of my back. Once in place, my arms stretched out over the jagged end until I felt the cloth catch onto the tip. Then I held my breath and pulled with the strength only desperation could give you. The sound of a satisfying rip bounced off the walls inside the tomb.

I wriggled my hands out of the loosened strips of cloth. The space was narrow, but I folded my knees to my chest as high as I could and untied the cloth rope around my ankles.

Like a worm, I wriggled down until my feet touched the rocks covering the opening of the tomb. A hard kick with my heel sent stones flying out. Puffs of dust wafted around me like clouds. I crawled out, feet first, into the blinding afternoon light. My wrists were sore and already bruised. Papa's watch. It was gone. It wasn't on the ground or inside the tomb I had been trapped in. Tiger must've taken it. My hand patted the pocket of my shorts. The money and balisong were still there. I sighed with relief. I adjusted the safety pin I kept on my shorts to keep my treasure from falling out.

What time was it? It felt like I had been trapped in the tomb for hours, but the sun was still high. There might still be a chance to save Jojo.

Ignoring my sore feet and an aching head, I raced home to find help. I prayed Mang Rudy was home. *Please, please, please.* I found little Ernie playing in the street with a hacky sack he had made with an old rag and pebbles. He ran up to me, his eyes wide with shock. "Nora, what happened to you? You're covered with cobwebs and mud. There's blood on your face too."

My hand went up automatically to touch my cheek.

It burned as I brushed at it. There was no time to think about my cuts and scratches.

"Is Mang Rudy home, Ernie? I need to talk to him."

"Yeah, come on!" He grabbed my hand and pulled me along toward Mang Rudy's grave house.

He was sitting at his work table with pieces of an electric fan he was trying to fix. He turned as we entered and stood, his stool clattering to the floor behind him.

"Susmaryosep! You're bleeding! What happened to you, Nora?" He peered at the scrapes on my face, the dust and dirt that covered every inch of me.

"It's Jojo! He needs help! Tiger and his gang tied him up and took him away!"

Mang Rudy held up his hand. "Slow down. Start from the beginning. Leave nothing out."

I told him about sneaking into Tiger's place, Jojo's kidnapping, and being thrown inside an empty tomb.

He listened while he located where his wife kept their box of medicines and bandages. He had me sit on top of his worktable and cleaned the dirt off my face, hands, and feet with a basin of clean water. He rubbed a little ointment on my scratches. When I complained about the lump on my head, he asked if I was dizzy or sleepy.

When I finished my story, he scowled and slapped a hand on his knee. "I told you to stay away from that cockroach. Well, I guess there's no point in scolding you now. We have to do something about Jojo."

I sipped water from a cup he handed to me. It hurt to

swallow. I rubbed my wrist, my heart aching from losing Papa's watch. Again.

Mang Rudy stood, plopped his baseball hat onto his head, and headed down the alley. Ernie and I were right on his heels when he turned and grabbed us both by the shoulders. "Now where do you think you're going?"

"I'm going with you," I said, surprised by the question.

He shook his head. "You've done enough. You go home and stay with your mother. I'm going to the police. Tiger's been in trouble before, so it shouldn't be hard to convince them to send some officers to Santiago's."

"But I can help. Please . . ."

"Nora, I mean it. Go home and stay with your mother. I'll send Virgil with a message as soon as I can."

Mang Rudy's son. He had been there that awful day when Tiger and his crew ransacked my grave house and stole Papa's watch. Ernie tugged at my hand as I stood there, my eyes fixed on Mang Rudy's rapidly retreating figure.

With heavy, painful steps, I turned and walked home. I wanted to help find Jojo. I needed to help find him. He wouldn't sit back and wait for someone else to find me if I were in his place. But I did need to check on Mama.

The singsong rhythm of Lola Mercy's voice drifted to me the closer I got to my grave house. I peered in and saw Lola sitting beside Mama, feeding her lagundi tea. Neither of them noticed me. I watched Lola, how her eyes crinkled when she smiled. I didn't take another step. I wouldn't, couldn't tell her that her one and only grandson was missing. I backed away and bumped into Ernie, almost knocking him down.

I had to find him myself. It was my fault he had gone to Tiger's in the first place. Mang Rudy was going to the police for help, but how long would it take them to get to Santiago's and save Jojo? It could take hours, and someone had to go there now, or it might be too late for Jojo. I could probably get there faster.

"Ernie, can I borrow your slippers?"

Without hesitating, he slipped them off his feet and handed them to me. "Can I help too, Nora?"

"You are going to help. Someone has to keep an eye on my mother and Jojo's lola, and you are the only one who can do it, okay?" With a quick kiss on his forehead, I ran to the cemetery gate with Ernie's too-small slippers on my sore feet.

Just then a motorcycle with a sidecar pulled up beside me. It was Virgil. He took a long look at my dirty clothes and bloody face. "Hey, I just dropped my father off at the police station. What's going on?"

Mang Rudy hadn't told him what happened. I climbed into the sidecar. "Do you know where Santiago's grocery store is?"

"Sure, but my father wanted me to tell you to stay home and wait for him to come back." He eyed the scratches on my face.

"Uh, yeah. But I need to buy some medicine for my mother." The half truth came out before I could stop myself.

"Yeah, I heard she wasn't well. Come on, then. I need to head out that way anyway to pick up my mother from the market." He would've probably refused to take me if he knew my real reason for going there.

The engine roared as we sped down the street, through the gate and into the stream of vehicles on Bonifacio Avenue. I chanted *Please hurry, please hurry* in my head, as if my will alone could make the motorcycle fly through the traffic.

I prayed I wasn't too late.

Chapter Twenty-six

"IF YOU LIKE, I CAN COME BACK FOR YOU AFTER I pick up my mother."

Virgil pulled up in front of Santiago's Grocery. He stopped by the entrance to let me out.

"Thank you. I'll wait for you on the sidewalk, by the street." If I could manage to find Jojo and sneak him out without getting caught, that is. Virgil waved goodbye and took off.

I got out of the way of customers coming in and out of the store and looked around. There seemed to be no unusual activity. It meant that Mang Rudy and the police weren't here yet.

I walked around the side of the building. The car I had

seen in front of Tiger's grave house was now parked in a space, right next to the back door. My heart thumped just a little harder as I walked up to the car and peeked in. There was no one inside. The door to the building was ajar. It creaked a little when I opened it.

The narrow hallway beyond was empty except for a pay phone set into a white-painted wall. I walked down the passage a few steps to the end, where there stood a stack of crates containing soda bottles. I peered around them and saw a large room with chairs set up in neat little rows. There were small tables topped with ashtrays and magazines at the end of each one. At the far end was a door with a sign that said *Ruel Santiago, President*. In front of it was a desk, where a woman was sitting with her back to me. There was a staircase on one side with a solid wooden rail that led to the second floor of the building.

Maybe I could sneak up the stairs without the secretary noticing. I took off Ernie's slippers. The cold floor felt good on my sore, scratched feet. I held my breath while I padded through the room, hoping no one noticed any bloody tracks I left behind. The woman at the desk was absorbed in something she was typing. I was halfway across when the door to Mr. Santiago's office swung open. I ducked behind a chair as the man with the pockmarked face and bulbous nose lumbered out.

"Chona, when you see Tiger, please tell him I have a meeting at City Hall and that I will deal with him and the boy when I get back." He closed his office door and locked it.

"Yes, sir. Before you leave, there is a contract you need to sign." The woman never looked up from her typing.

Mr. Santiago waved dismissively, golden rings gleaming on his hands, and left through another door. A machine on the woman's desk whirred. Sheets of paper rolled out of an opening and fell into a tray. She gathered the papers, grabbed a pen, and followed her boss out through the same door.

After making sure there was no one else around, I dashed for the stairs and climbed up. The second-floor hallway was empty and quiet except for some low voices coming from the end of the corridor. I ducked into a nearby doorway when Tiger and one of his friends stepped out of a room down the hall.

"Will it be okay to leave this guy here by himself? I thought the boss said to watch him." It was the skinny one. He was like a mosquito that kept turning up to bite you in the leg again and again.

Tiger shook his head and touched his nose gingerly. "He'll be fine. He's tied up and gagged, where is he going to go? I'm going to the restroom to clean up what that other brat did to my nose." They walked down the hall, past my hiding place, to the stairs.

When I was sure they were gone, I ran to the room they'd come out of. It was some kind of storage space, just like the one I had hidden in. There were shelves with boxes that had *PURE FOODS* and *SILVER SWAN* stamped on them. Crates were also stacked on the floor next to a table that had a clipboard and rolls of tape piled on top.

There seemed to be no one in the room. Maybe Jojo was somewhere else.

As I turned to leave, I heard a muffled cry from behind a stack of flattened cardboard boxes. Jojo was lying on the floor. My knees went weak and I collapsed next to him. I pulled the gag out of his mouth.

"What do you think you're doing?" Jojo asked in a hoarse whisper. "Do you realize what danger you're putting yourself in?" His eyes were wide, shifting between the open door and me. His lips compressed into a thin line. "Help me out of these ropes. They'll be back soon."

I pulled the balisong out of my pocket. It cut easily through the ropes tied around his wrists and ankles. "Thanks," he said, examining the marks they left on his skin. His spiky hair was matted on one side and his right eye and cheek were bruised and puffy. He looked me over. "What in the world happened to you?"

"I'll tell you later. We have to get out of here first. Virgil is going to pick us up, so we have to hurry." I gestured toward the door. Jojo came up behind me and we both listened for returning footsteps.

It was quiet. Maybe Tiger and his gang had left. We came out into the hallway. My legs shook as we walked down the staircase. My breath caught in my throat when I heard Tiger and Chona talking from an open door across the way. Tiger stood with his back facing us while Chona pointed to a memo tacked to the wall.

Jojo and I sat on the stairs behind the rail. With a hand

cupped over Jojo's ear, I whispered, "We'll have to leave through the back door, which is around that corner over there." The bend in the hall was right in front of us.

"I remember. That was the door they carried me through earlier," Jojo whispered back with a grimace. "We better move fast."

Together, Jojo and I tiptoed into the hallway. I kept looking back to watch for Tiger, ready to make a break for it, when I bumped into the stack of crates. The sound of rattling bottles echoed down the corridor. I pushed on the stack to steady them just as one of Tiger's henchmen walked in through the back door.

"Hoy!" He lunged after us. We turned and ran the other way. Tiger ran out of the room across the stairs and blocked our escape.

I grabbed an ashtray from a nearby table and threw it at him. When he ducked to avoid it, Jojo and I dodged past him. We ran up the stairs. Tiger and his friend pounded up the steps behind us.

"We can escape through there," panted Jojo.

He ran to a window at the end of the hallway that I hadn't noticed before. It was large with two rectangular panes of glass. There were levers on one side of the window that could be turned so that it swung outward as it opened.

"We're going to have to jump. Give me the balisong. I'll try to hold them off while you crank the window open," commanded Jojo. With the balisong in his hand, I watched as he flicked it open and held it out. He was ready to fight.

Tiger and his buddy stopped a few feet away from us. I froze. They stared at Jojo with new eyes as he pointed the balisong at them.

"Open the window," said Jojo through gritted teeth, not taking his eyes off the enemy in front of him. He slashed the knife through the air whenever they moved.

My body finally unfroze and, with shaking hands, I grabbed hold of a metal lever. It wouldn't turn. The window wouldn't budge no matter how hard I pushed. A hiss escaped through my clenched teeth when I noticed a small latch at the bottom of the window. I lifted it and the lever turned with ease. The window swung open in front of me. Customers milled around in front of the entrance below. Virgil was already parked on the curb, talking to his mother.

"Virgil!" I screamed his name. He turned his head toward the sound of my voice. Just then, there was a scuffle behind me and a sharp intake of breath. The skinny man held his hand over a cut on his cheek. It bled freely through his fingers. Jojo swung the knife at him again and then at Tiger. Sooner or later, they were going to figure out how to overpower Jojo. We had to get out. The only way was down. But how? Below the window was a folded metal ladder. With a hard pull, the fire escape unfolded and slid all the way to the concrete below.

"Let's go!" I had one leg over the windowsill when Jojo grunted and bumped me from behind. They were all on the floor, with Tiger holding Jojo down while the other thug pried the knife out of Jojo's hand.

"Jojo!" My eyes scanned around wildly for a way to help him. There was a small room on my right, lined with shelves full of toilet paper and plastic bottles. There was a broom standing in the corner. I grabbed it and whacked the skinny man's back over and over. He turned and grabbed the broom from my hands and pushed me away. I backed into the storage room as he came toward me. I reached out and clamped on to the first thing my hand touched. A plastic spray bottle.

"Come on, throw it at me," dared the man, grinning with stained, crooked teeth.

I was going to do just that when the pink liquid sloshing inside the bottle gave me another idea. I aimed straight for his eyes. My fingers pumped the trigger fast and hard. The fluid came out in a fine mist that smelled like the cleaner Aling Lydia used to spray on the windows of the bakery. The man waved off the mist as he stumbled backward but I kept on spraying. He coughed violently and then screamed when the cleaner trickled into his eyes.

Jojo and Tiger continued grappling on the floor. They were both covered with cuts from the balisong, which Tiger finally knocked out of Jojo's hand and kicked away. Tiger was trying to reach for the knife, but Jojo kept wrestling him back. He looked surprised by Jojo's strength. He was, after all, only a thirteen-year-old boy who hauled water from the water pump every day.

Just as Tiger's hand came within a millimeter of the balisong, I grabbed it before he could take hold of it. Then something else caught my eye. Papa's watch was on the floor by the stairs. Tiger must have dropped it during the fight. I scrambled for it. When I had it, I kissed it, slipped it over my hand, and closed the clasp.

"Nora!"

Tiger had Jojo in a headlock. Then he pinned Jojo to the floor and punched him over and over in the head.

With the balisong in one hand, I pointed the spray bottle at Tiger's face with the other and pumped the trigger a few times. He reeled back and fell against the wall. He shielded his face with one hand and tried to wipe the stinging liquid from his eyes with the other. I continued to pump the trigger until Jojo stood once again, wiping the blood from his nose with the end of his T-shirt.

Tiger squirmed on the floor and screamed, "My eyes! You blinded me, you little witch! Ahhh!"

Over his screams came the sound of many feet coming up the stairs. Mang Rudy, Virgil, and a couple of policemen rushed toward us.

The policemen's eyes traveled from the two men moaning on the floor, to Jojo's bloody nose and bruised face, and lastly, to me with a balisong in one hand and a half-empty spray bottle of pink window cleaner in the other.

Chapter Twenty-seven

"Did they arrest him?" Mama's voice was getting stronger each day. The color of her face was warm, her lips had a pink flush to them, and her eyes sparkled.

"Yes, they did. They're charging him with kidnapping and something called extortion."

"And what about Mr. Santiago?"

"Mr. Santiago found out that Tiger had been stealing from him as well. The police chief is his friend, so Tiger and his gang will be in jail for a long time."

Mama had been in the hospital for five days now. The doctor who treated her said that we got her to the hospital just in time. Her infection had gone into her blood and she would've died without the right kind of medicine. She still had some pain, but at least her fever was gone. The only concern now was how her illness had affected her heart. The infection weakened it, so she had to stay for observation. I guessed that meant they wanted to keep an eye on her. The doctor tried to explain this to me so that I could understand. Mama would have to come back to see him in a month to make sure her heart was doing fine.

Mama lay in a charity ward with ten beds. The room had other patients there, but it was comfortable and the nurses were friendly.

The first two days at the hospital were the hardest. The doctors cleaned Mama's wound and stuck a tube into her arm that connected to a plastic bag of liquid that contained medicine for the infection and something like vitamins. The nurses tried to make me leave with Lola Mercy and Mang Rudy, saying it was no place for a child, but I refused to let go of my mother's hand. They finally let me stay and even brought out a small cot for me to sleep on. Mama had slept most of the last five days, but today, she was able to sit up. She even looked younger because her cheeks were a little puffy. According to the doctor, it was because of the liquid that was slowly dripping into her veins from the bag suspended over her head.

Mama reached out for my hand, squeezed it, and turned it over to look at the blue-and-silver face of Papa's watch. "It was nice of Mang Rudy to fix the band so you could wear it. Are you going to tell me what happened?"

Yesterday she had asked me about it, but Aling Lydia

had come to visit and stayed so long and had so much to say that she wore Mama out. I wasn't looking forward to telling her what had happened with Tiger, but she deserved to know.

"Well, I guess I should start at the beginning." The story of how Tiger took the watch the day after she disappeared, and everything that had happened afterward, came out in bits and pieces. It was as if my soul did not want to share the longing, pain, and loneliness of those moments when she had gone missing. But I did share it. Even the scary parts. And together we cried over it all.

"I have failed you, Nora. Over and over again. If it weren't for me, your father would still be alive." Mama pressed her hand to her mouth, holding back a wail that curled her body into a ball. She shook, tears pouring from her eyes, filling creases and folds until they streamed over her hands.

My own eyes, already puffy from crying, began tearing up again. "Don't say that, Mama, please." I twisted away from her, wiping my eyes.

"It's true. I have to say this." She took my hands in hers, forcing me to face her. Mama bent her head and pressed her lips to my fingers. She stayed like that for a long time and when she finally looked up, her face was calm, her eyes steely with determination. "Did you ever wonder why Papa went back into the house to find me when I was already outside?"

I blinked, my breath caught in my throat. "No. I thought

you got out while Papa came to get me, and he didn't know that you had escaped."

A heavy pressure began in the middle of my chest. It felt like someone was pressing a finger against it, harder and harder. I didn't know if I wanted to hear what Mama had to say. One thing seemed clear, though. Mama needed to speak the truth.

"Your father and I had an argument. I wanted to play mahjong with my friend at a wake. I thought, since it was a Friday, and your father didn't have work the next day, it would be okay to go." Mama closed her eyes, her lip trembling. "He didn't want me to leave. He said I'd been playing too much. I went to the kitchen, pretending to clean up. You were already asleep and after half an hour, I heard your father snoring. That was when I snuck out."

I stared, her blurred image coming into focus again when I blinked away my tears. She was crying too, her eyes wide and confused, staring into the past.

"I heard the sirens. People were running. I wasn't too far away; the funeral home was only a few blocks down the street. I saw the smoke and the glow of orange against the black sky. I ran. There was already a crowd of people around our apartment building. The flames were too big and other houses had begun to catch fire. I saw your father run into our unit, calling my name . . ."

"Oh, Mama." I didn't know what to think or say.

Mama sighed. "Gambling became my comfort. I knew I was getting out of control, but I'd tell myself that it was all going to work out and that I was doing it all to get us out of the cemetery, to go home to Davao—gambling is an addiction. I can see that now."

I pulled her hands to my chest. "I will help you, Mama!"

"Oh, anak, you've done so much. I lost almost all our washing jobs, but you held on to the one we had with Aling Lydia. You sold garlands to keep us fed when all I could think about was winning my next game of mahjong." She pulled me into her arms. "I let you down. I let Papa down. I made a promise to take care of you. I've made so many bad choices. Can you possibly forgive me?"

Sobs crowded my throat and prevented any words from escaping. I wanted to tell her that, yes, I forgave her. And more than that, I wanted to ask her for forgiveness.

"I'm sorry too, Mama."

"For what, anak?"

"I'm not sure. I guess for not trusting you more. I thought you left me."

"What? Oh, I would never leave you." She squeezed me tight and kissed the tears from my face. "Things will be different from now on. Aling Lydia offered to give me my washing job back, but since I can't lift anything for a while, she offered me a job in the bakery instead. She will teach me how to make pandesal. In fact, she wants both of us to work there. I will work in the kitchen and you can work behind the counter. We'll save money, and I promise, no more mahjong!"

Mama was going to work in the bakery? What would

Perla think of that? I was going to joke around with Mama and ask her if Aling Lydia would let her take home some bread, when a familiar voice echoed through the big room.

"Lorna? Which bed would she be in? Ay! I'm sorry! I'm looking for my friend."

Mama's eyes brightened. "Rosie! I'm over here!"

Rosie saw us just as I jumped off Mama's bed. She looked a little shy walking through the ward, carrying a plastic bag filled with small green fruit.

"Kumusta? I brought you some guavas. I know they're your favorite."

"Salamat. This is my daughter, Nora. Oh, that's right, you two have already met. How did you know I was in the hospital?"

"Oh, well, I ran into Nora's friend, Jojo. He told me you were here. My uncle is in the hospital as well."

Rosie couldn't stay for very long and promised to visit Mama again before she was discharged from the hospital. Her visit reminded me of something.

"Why did you decide to use Rosie's address when you wrote to Tito Danny?"

Her brow wrinkled. She smoothed the bedsheet over her thighs and sighed.

"You do remember that I was writing to him because I sold my cell phone? Well, at first, the return address I used was Lola Fely's. I would go to her house and ask if I had any mail. She told me each time I came by that I didn't have any. Dina told me later on that he did write to us, only Lola Fely hid the letters."

"What? Why would she want to hide them from us?" It was a shocking thing to acknowledge, even though it was something I'd suspected from the start.

"Who knows? That woman did everything she could to make our lives miserable. She never had an ounce of compassion for us, especially since she believed that my marriage to your father was the cause of her brother's— your grandfather's—death." Mama rubbed her temples as if thoughts of Lola Fely pained her.

"So how did you figure it all out?" So there was more to the story than she had let on before.

"Rosie encouraged me to write to Tito Danny again. She let me use her house for the return address. It's a good thing she did or he wouldn't have been able to contact us. Dina told me that my brother called Lola Fely once to ask about us, but she refused to come to the phone." She rubbed my hands as she spoke. It felt good to be consoled, though for some reason I couldn't explain, I didn't feel disappointed. There was a time when this news would've blasted all my hopes of escaping the cemetery. It seemed like a long time ago.

Mama went on. "Well, as you can imagine, I was so angry with Lola Fely that I wanted to storm over to her house and tell her exactly what I thought of her, her money and family. But instead, I tried to ask her for a loan. When she refused, I did tell her what I thought of her. We don't need her, Nora."

"We don't. But you went to see Tiger."

She squeezed my hand and turned her face away. The tears were already spilling over onto her cheeks. "Yes. Rosie told me about him, how she met him and how he harassed her. I think he was a little in love with her. Anyway, her uncle had borrowed money from Mr. Santiago before. Rosie asked Tiger to set up an appointment for me to see him."

"So this is Rosie's fault!"

"No, Nora. I owed money to a few of my friends. I couldn't go back to Lola Fely after I found out she hid Tito Danny's letters from me. She couldn't be trusted anyway after swindling me out of Papa's savings. I told Rosie that I was desperate. That was how I met Tiger and Mr. Santiago." Mama closed her eyes and sighed, the sound catching a little in her throat. "I knew how much you wanted to leave the cemetery, to live in a real home again. I must confess that the thought of going back to Davao, having a new home, a chance for you to go back to school, made me so excited. I didn't consider what would happen if I couldn't pay Mr. Santiago back." A tear trickled down her cheek and landed on my hand.

"I know, Mama." The reasons why she did what she did didn't really matter to me anymore. I was just glad she was alive. "I was ashamed, Mama, I can see that now. I don't feel that way anymore. We will do the best we can with what we have. I'll take the job at the bakery and sell garlands. We'll be all right as long as we're together. Besides, I'm not sure I want to leave Manila anymore. In a way, Lola and Jojo have become our family. He's been like a brother to me. And you know what? I'm teaching him how to read. He knows some basics but I'll have lots to teach him. Also, if we move to Davao, we'd be far from Papa."

"But anak, we can't possibly find another home here. I want you to go back to school."

Me too. More than anything. My thoughts drifted back to the book and the scholarship papers Kuya Efren had given to me.

I told her about the forms and that Kuya Efren had written a recommendation letter for me. This made Mama's eyes fill with tears again. I promised to show her the papers as soon as she got home.

"The doctor says they will release you tomorrow, Mama. I'll be going home in a little while to get things ready and to bring back some clothes for you to wear."

Mama smiled wistfully, happy to get back to a normal routine. Then she frowned again, the worry-crease between her brows deepening. "Will you be coming back tonight?"

"No, I'll be back tomorrow with your clothes. I have to wash our things and sweep out the grave house. But don't worry, I won't spend the night at home by myself. I'll stay with Lola, and Jojo will sleep at our place."

"Hey, I heard someone say my name!" Jojo peeked around the divider at us. It was him, but it wasn't him. For one thing, his hair was combed, held down with so much pomade it made his hair look like a helmet. He was wearing blue jeans, an old sports shirt, and a clean pair of sneakers.

The shock at his appearance must've been so clear on my face that he looked embarrassed. He stood there looking at Mama, then at me, scratching the back of his head so hard, he made the hair behind his head stick up like a rooster's tail.

"Where are you going? I've never seen you so *clean* before." A small bubble of laughter popped out of my chest. I put a hand over my mouth to stop it. I didn't want to embarrass him more.

"And with real clothes on? Yeah, I know, I look a little weird. But I'm going to a job interview and Mang Rudy said that I should at least wear pants and comb my hair." He smoothed back the rooster tail on top of his head and smiled.

"Really? What's the interview for?" This was really good news. Anything was better than hauling water. Almost anything. People did desperate things to survive, which I remembered only too well.

"Here. The nurse told me they needed someone to do things like sweep the floors and empty trash cans. She thinks I'm sixteen years old." He chuckled and then glanced at the clock on the wall nearby. "Oh, I'm going to be late! Tita Lorna, sorry to leave so quickly. I'll be back for Nora as soon as I'm done."

Jojo's voice echoed as he left the room, causing a grumpy

patient to shush him and mutter a complaint. Mama and I looked at each other and smiled. Then we giggled until Mama held her side. "What a great young man Jojo will be. Now, aren't you glad he's your friend?"

"Yes, Mama." I rested my head in her lap while she stroked my hair. I closed my eyes, listening to her breathing, the soft murmur of other voices in the ward, and the rustle of sheets when Mama shifted her feet. It felt so good to lie there, I nearly drifted off to sleep. Then Mama tapped me lightly on the cheek. I opened my eyes.

"Do you think Jojo will come back after his interview?" asked Mama.

I sat up and stretched. "I hope he does. He's supposed to accompany me home."

"You know, I had a good feeling about Jojo since I met him that first day we moved to the cemetery. He was so eager to help us, even when you did your best to snub him. I'm so thankful for his lola's friendship as well. He looked smart all dressed up like that, didn't he?"

I smiled, hoping with all my heart that he would get the job. He was a true friend, my very best friend.

"Yeah, I guess so."

Jojo came up behind me. "Who's smart?"

I jumped. I spun around and glared at him. "Jojo! It's very rude to eavesdrop."

Mama giggled behind me. With supreme effort, I tried to keep a straight face. "I thought you went to your interview!"

"I did. The head of housekeeping was just down the hall. We talked a little and she told me I could start tomorrow! Hey, I don't want to rush you, but we should get going before it gets dark." He waved to Mama and went out into the hall to wait for me.

"I'm so happy for him, Mama. It seems like things are looking better for everyone." Mama simply nodded and smiled gently. She looked tired now, so I kissed her good-night and left.

Tomorrow, Mama would finally be home.

Home.

It didn't feel so bad to say that now.

Chapter Twenty-eight

THE REST OF THAT DAY AND MOST OF THE NEXT morning were spent washing clothes, sweeping out the grave house, and shaking out our sleeping mats. I even had time to go buy some food and supplies with the money we had left over after paying for Mama's doctor's bill. Rosie had returned to visit Mama with a letter from Tito Danny. He apologized for not returning my first call. Mang Rudy's phone number was unfamiliar and he had been wary about calling it. It turned out he hadn't received my message at all. When I called him again and told him about Mama's illness, he was glad he had answered the phone this time. The letter said he had sold one of his carabaos and a few pigs to pay for her treatment and hospital stay, and included instructions on where to pick up the money. Mang Rudy had accompanied me.

Jojo had taught me how important it was to tell your friends the truth. I had learned that the hard way. It was why I decided to call Evelyn and tell her everything that had happened to my mother and me. She came to the hospital with some fruit for Mama and a book for me. She promised to pass by Ibarra bakery once a week so we could catch up. I would start working tomorrow.

Tiger had confessed to the police about stealing goods from Mr. Santiago's store. He also confessed to cheating Mama out of the money his boss had paid for the extra work she had done in the factory.

I used some of that money to pay for medicines that Mama needed when she came home. There was enough left for food and my stock of everlasting daisies for a few weeks. My uncle promised us a small bamboo house of our own and a pig to raise if we decided to come and live in Davao someday.

"Someday seems like a long way away, Papa. I guess you're stuck with us for now."

Everything was ready for Mama's homecoming. A necklace of sweet-smelling sampaguita hung around our Santo Niño statue in thanksgiving. Mama's clothes and slippers were packed. Virgil and his tricycle would take me to the hospital to pick her up this afternoon.

While I waited for my ride, I decided to make a few everlasting-daisy garlands to decorate Papa's tomb, when

I remembered the potted plant in the corner. I picked it up to throw it out when I noticed a bundle of clothes on top of the dead sweet potato plant. It was the shirt and shorts I'd worn the last time I saw Tiger. They were stained and still smelled of the tomb he'd thrown me into.

I wanted to throw them away, to not have any more reminders of how close I came to losing everything that was important to me. But then again, it might be a good reminder of what *not* to do for the sake of money, and how to never, ever again lose hope.

The crusted dirt fell away like sand when I shook the shorts. Something fell out of the pocket. It was a folded piece of yellow paper, worn and ragged at the edges.

It was the flyer about the St. Anne's Academy scholarship, the one Jojo had given me a few days ago. The image of the little nun talking to Aling Lydia flashed through my mind and my heart gave a hopeful skip.

Strange—all my desire for escape was gone. All I could think about now was filling out the forms for the scholarship to St. Anne's. I had worked on my review book while I sat by Mama's hospital bed. I was almost done. Kuya Efren had already given me a recommendation letter. Aling Lydia would let me have Perla's old uniforms. I could study while I worked behind the counter at Aling Lydia's bakery.

It was really going to happen. I could go back to school.

I found the bag containing the review book and my scholarship application forms. The convent and school were close by; I could drop it off one day after work.

I refolded the yellow paper and tucked it next to Mama's clothes so I could show it to her. I was stuffing the smelly clothes in a plastic bag to wash later on when something odd caught my eye. A small green leaf poked up out of the debris of dried stems and leaves in the pot. *It's still alive!* I cleaned the dirt around it and poured water over the plant. Then I positioned it to catch some sunlight, thinking about roasted sweet potatoes and how much Mama loved them.

The distant hum of a motorcycle became a roar as it neared my grave house. It was time to leave.

"Let's go, Nora!" Jojo rode behind Virgil on the motor-cycle, letting me have the sidecar.

With Mama's clothes under my arm, I climbed in with a heart that was light, happy, and filled with hope. As we pulled away, I realized that my grave house looked brighter. Rays of sunshine reflected off the painted white cement of Papa's tomb. The old plastic table gleamed with a pretty flower design that I'd never noticed before. Our worn but brightly colored checkered mat and the gauzy lightness of the kulambo were neatly stacked in the corner. The shad-ows of sadness were gone and all that remained were the odds and ends of our daily lives.

Mama was coming home.

Glossary
of Tagalog Words

*** ALL VOWELS ARE SHORT ***

ADOBO (a-do-bo) – a chicken or pork stew cooked in soy sauce and vinegar.

ALING (a-ling) – a title of respect used before the first name of a woman.

ALIS (a-lis) – scram, go, remove.

ANAK (a-nak) – child, daughter/son.

ARAY (a-rye) – an expression meaning "ouch!"

BAHALA NA (ba-ha-la na) – an expression meaning "come what may."

BALISONG (ba-li-song) – a butterfly knife.

BANANA-QUE (ba-na-na-kyu) – plantains deep-fried in caramelized sugar; a street food sold on skewers.

BANIG (ba-nig) – a woven mat.

BARONG TAGALOG (ba-rong ta-ga-log) – an embroidered formal shirt considered the national dress of the Philippines.

BIKO (bee-ko) – a rice cake.

BRUHA (bru-ha) – witch, old hag.

BULI (boo-li) – a kind of palm leaf.

CALAMANSI (ka-la-man-si) – a sour fruit also known as calamondin; an intergenetic hybrid of citrus fruit and kumquats.

CAPIZ SHELLS (ka-piz) – they come from windowpane oysters.

CARABAO (ka-ra-bow) – a water buffalo.

CHAMPORADO (cham-po-ra-do) – a porridge made with glutinous rice, cocoa, milk, and sugar.

CHOW (chow) – a mahjong rule when a player has a numerical series of three tiles all of the same suit.

CONSUELO (con-swe-lo) – consolation.

DAPA (da-pa) – bend over.

DINUGUAN (di-nu-guan) – a pork stew made with pork blood.

DIWATA (di-wa-ta) – fairy or goddess.

GINATAAN (gi-na-tan) – a warm dessert made with sticky rice balls and coconut cream.

HAYOP KA (ha-yop ka) – a rude expression meaning "you animal."

HINDE, HINDI (hin-de, hin-di) – an expression meaning "no," "not."

HOY (hoi) – an expression meaning "hey."

JEEPNEY (jeep-ney) – a common form of public transportation; an extended jeep with colorful decorations; a symbol of Philippine culture and art.

KONG (kong) – a mahjong rule when a player has four matching tiles.

KULAMBO (ku-lam-bo) – mosquito net.

KUMUSTA (ku-mus-ta) – hello, regards. "Kumusta ka?" means "How are you?"

KUYA (ku-ya) – older brother; a term of address or reference.

LABANDERA (la-ban-de-ra) – laundrywoman who washes clothes by hand.

LAGUNDI (la-gun-di) – a shrub that grows in the Philippines. It is used in herbal medicine.

LOLA (lo-la) – grandmother; a term of address or reference.

LUGAW (lu-gau) – a rice porridge.

MAGANDANG UMAGA (ma-gan-dang u-ma-ga) – good morning.

MANG (mang) – a title of respect used before the first name of a man.

NAKU (na-ku) – an expression that can mean "oh, my."

NASAAN KA? (na-san ka) – where are you?

PALANGGANA (pa-lan-ga-na) – a basin.

PALENGKE (pa-leng-ke) – marketplace.

PANCIT CANTON (pan-cit kan-ton) – a Filipino noodle dish with vegetables, pork, chicken, and shrimp.

PANDESAL (pan-de-sal) – a common bread roll in the Philippines.

PASOK (pa-sok) – enter.

PO (po) – an expression that indicates respect or politeness.

PONG (pong) – a mahjong rule when a player has a set of three matching tiles.

PUHUNAN (pu-hu-nan) – capital for business.

SABA (sa-ba) – a common cooking banana.

SALAMAT (sa-la-mat) – thanks, thank you.

SALOMPAS (sa-lom-pas) – a topical pain reliever in patch form.

SANDALI LANG (san-da-li lang) – an expression meaning "just a moment, just a minute."

SANTOL (san-tol) – a tropical sour fruit.

SARI-SARI (sa-ri-sa-ri) – variety; a sari-sari store sells a variety of goods.

SEMENTERYO (se-men-te-ri-yo) – cemetery.

SIGE NA (si-ge na) – an expression meaning "go on now."

SINIGANG (si-ni-gang) – a soup made of tamarind, meat or fish, and vegetables.

SIYEMPRE (siyem-pre) – always, of course, surely, naturally.

SUMAN (su-man) – a steamed rice cake wrapped in banana or palm leaf.

SUSMARYOSEP (sus-mar-yo-sep) – an expression; a combination of Jesus, Mary, Joseph.

SUWERTE (su-wer-te) – luck; good luck; good fortune.

TITA (tee-ta) – aunt; a term of address or reference.

TITO (tee-to) – uncle; a term of address or reference.

TRICYCLE – an auto-rickshaw, motorcycle with a sidecar, a common form of public transportation in the Philippines.

TURO-TURO (tu-ro tu-ro) – a cafeteria-style restaurant.

WALANG ANUMAN (wa-lang a-nu-man) – not at all.

WALIS TINGTING (wa-lis ting-ting) – a broom made from the dried midribs of a coconut.

Author's Note

Everlasting Nora is a work of fiction, but the telling of this tale is inspired by real children living in extreme poverty in Manila.

I was born in the Philippines, but when my family moved to the United States, I grew up without any novels about Filipino children like me. When I returned to my native country, I celebrated my first All Saints' Day as a curious twelve-year-old girl. The cemetery was crowded with colorful, decorated tombs and mausoleums. There were lots of people there that day, visitors like me, and lots of vendors selling food and candles. It was quite festive!

But I had no idea there were people actually *living* there.

After college, I moved back to the United States. I loved to read, and when my children were born, I wanted them to have books they could see themselves in. I had planned to write a picture book based on my memory of my first All Saints' Day in the Philippines, when my cousins showed me how to make balls by collecting melted wax from the candles burning around the tombs. I began my online research on Philippine cemeteries and Filipino traditions surrounding honoring the dead.

I first learned about the homeless living in cemeteries when I came across a blog post written by a Baptist missionary who had traveled to the Philippines. He wrote about a girl named Grace, an orphan living in the Manila North Cemetery, who begged in the streets to stay alive. The missionary was moved by her plight. It alarmed him that there were so many children like her. He returned home and raised money to open a safe house for orphaned, homeless children like Grace. He came back to the Philippines with volunteers to help rescue these children. He searched for Grace but learned that she had died in a charity hospital, alone. I was so touched by her story I decided I wanted to write about a girl like her and I knew it had to be a novel. *Everlasting Nora* took shape and became the book you now hold in your hands.

Just like the character Nora, hundreds of poor families live in cemeteries. Many children who live there were born there, just like their parents and grandparents. Some of the homeless work as caretakers for families who own graves and mausoleums; others sell peanuts or roasted corn to cemetery visitors or other homeless people. They make enough money to buy the simplest necessities. Some of the children even go to school. But most do not. Like Nora, they lack the money to buy uniforms and school supplies.

Efren Peñaflorida, a Filipino teacher and social worker, inspired the character Kuya Efren Pena. He was one of the founding members of Dynamic Teen Company, a youth group dedicated to community activism. He became CNN's Hero of the Year in 2009 for his efforts to bring education to children who live in slums and cemeteries.

The Dynamic Teen Company continues their mission of outreach by bringing education to impoverished children and providing guidance to teens to become productive members of their community. You can read more about them at dtc.org.ph.

Gawad Kalinga is an organization whose mission is to end poverty in the Philippines by providing ways to build sustainability in very poor communities all over the country. They help build houses for homeless people who live in cemeteries and polluted slums. Their vision has reached other countries like Cambodia and Indonesia. You can learn more about them at gk1world.com/home.

If you would like to read some reference articles I studied in order to portray my characters respectfully, please go to my website: cruzwrites.com/for-teachers.html.

Thank you for taking this journey with my characters, whose lives reflect real humans who find the courage to stay alive and keep their families safe through the strength of their communities.

Everlasting Nora

BY MARIE MIRANDA CRUZ
Ages 8–12; Grades 3–7

With a narrative that weaves between the past and present, *Everlasting Nora* is a bittersweet story of both losing and finding precious things. Forced to live as a squatter in the Philippines' Manila North Cemetery after an apartment fire destroys her home and takes her father's life, Nora, the story's vulnerable but resilient young narrator, is already struggling with devastating loss when her mother goes missing. Nora's fears for Mama's welfare, and her own, escalate when a loan shark's thugs intimidate Nora; steal her savings and her beloved Papa's watch; and deliver the distressing news that Mama, who has built up debt from a gambling problem, owes their unforgiving boss money. With surprising support from her cemetery neighbors, whose pockets are empty but hearts are full, Nora marshals the courage to find Mama, recover Papa's watch, earn money, and get Mama to a hospital for life-saving care. Through her harrowing journey of change and loss, Nora finds that some things, like a parent's love, true friendship, inner strength, hope, and memories, are enduring, maybe even everlasting.

Reading *Everlasting Nora* with Your Children
PRE-READING DISCUSSION QUESTIONS

1. In *Everlasting Nora*, the main character, Nora, has to drop out of school because of unfortunate circumstances in her life.

She and her mother are forced to make a makeshift residence in the cemetery, where other struggling families also use mausoleums, or grave houses protecting tombs, as their homes. Looking back on her old, familiar life, Nora misses things she used to take for granted, even things she once might have complained about, like math class. Have you ever experienced a loss or change that gave you new appreciation for the importance of someone or something? Or, what are some things you have in your life today that you value, even if you don't always think about how lucky you are to have them? What would you miss most if you couldn't have it or do it? Why?

2. When Nora and Mama find themselves living as squatters in the Manila North Cemetery, Nora hides a shoebox with her most precious possessions in their grave house. The box contains a picture of Nora with Mama and Papa, who tragically lost his life in the fire that destroyed their home; her papa's wristwatch; and her savings, which she hopes will help her return to a real home and school someday. If you had to put three objects in a cardboard box to represent three of the most important things in your life, what would you choose, and why? Where would you keep the box? Do you think the items you'd pick to put in the box today would be the same things you would have picked to put in the box a year ago? Why or why not?

POST-READING DISCUSSION QUESTIONS

1. *Everlasting Nora* opens with title character Nora's thoughts about what home does and doesn't mean: "If someone were to ask me to describe a home, I would tell them this. A home never floods during a typhoon. A home has a kitchen with a stove for cooking rice. A home does not have dead people inside it." How

would you "fill in" these blanks for yourself and your idea of home, and why would you give the answers you do?

A home never . . . A home has . . . A home does not have . . .

2. Throughout the novel, Nora observes many contrasts in her life and surroundings. For example, when Nora is walking home from selling everlasting-daisy garlands at the cemetery gates, she is keenly aware of differences between herself, a cemetery *resident*, and the visitors to the cemetery. Can you think of other contrasts, or juxtapositions (very different things close to each other, making the differences even more apparent), from the story?

3. Living as a squatter in the cemetery, Nora misses her best friend, Evelyn, a classmate from her old school, but says she wouldn't want Evelyn to see her now. Why?

4. Author Marie Miranda Cruz incorporates words from the Tagalog language, but uses "context clues" to help readers figure out what the foreign words mean. For example, Nora says "salamat" ("thanks" or "thank you") when outreach teacher Kuya Efren invites her to continue a lesson. Did you "translate" Tagalog words using context clues? (Use the book's Glossary to double-check your guesses.)

5. Nora cherishes Papa's watch as a precious link to his memory. The watch itself is important in the story, but can it also be seen as a symbol for some of the bigger themes, or important ideas, such as time, memory, and the relationship between past and present, emphasized throughout the novel? In the "story of Papa's watch," for example, the old man (whom Papa's father helps) leaves the watch and a note, thanking Papa's father for

having helped save the old man's memories. Why do you think the memories are so precious?

6. In Chapter Three, Nora says Mama is "sick" with "gambling-itis." What does Nora think about Mama playing all-night mahjong games? Does it sometimes seem like the mother and daughter roles are reversed with Mama and Nora? How does that make Nora feel?

7. What do we learn about the "Holy Week" fire in Chapter Four? After the fire, Nora and Mama go to stay with Papa's aunt, Lola Fely. How does her treatment of Nora and Mama change over time? What does Lola Fely reveal about how Nora's parents met, and what does this information make Nora realize about her mother's relationship, and her own, with Lola Fely and Papa's cousins?

8. What does Tiger tell Nora during the confrontation in her grave house, and what does Tiger steal? In Chapter Five, in the aftermath of Tiger's break-in, Nora observes: "I gazed, numb inside, at the clothes strewn on the floor and at the bruised leaves of my sweet potato plant." Throughout the story, Nora monitors the condition of her cherished sweet potato plant. Does the plant's struggle to survive, even flourish, in punishing conditions mirror Nora's own journey? Can you think of examples from the story that illustrate this?

9. In Chapter Six, Nora describes meeting good-natured Jojo for the first time, and wondering: "Who did this boy think he was? And why was he so at ease in a place like this?" Why is Nora surprised by Jojo's attitude? Why is Nora cautious about becoming friends with Jojo?

10. Mama tells Nora early in the story that Papa's spirit will watch over them and come to them if they need it, but only in dreams. In Chapter Eight, Nora dreams about Papa's watch "crumbling to ash." What do you think the dream means?

11. When she is back, Mama tells Nora about going to Lola Fely to ask for a loan. How does that visit lead to Mama complaining about money troubles to her mahjong friend Rosie and borrowing money from Tiger's boss, Mr. Santiago?

12. In Chapter Nineteen, Jojo tells Nora: "Kids who live in the cemetery care and want the same things you do, but they're like me. They live day to day. We are happy to be alive, to have something to eat and a place to sleep. We say, bahala na! Come what may! It will be too depressing, otherwise. Maybe the other kids keep their distance because you remind them of what they *should* be thinking about." Whose approach do you think is more effective for navigating cemetery life, Nora's or Jojo's? Why?

13. To comfort Mama while she's ill, Nora reads her "A Tree with No Name: The Legend of the Mango Tree." In spite of being nameless and unable to bear fruit, the tree is kind, and a magical creature rewards its compassion by giving it fruit and a name. Can you cite examples from *Everlasting Nora* where Jojo, Lola Mercy, Little Ernie, Mang Rudy, or other cemetery squatters' attitude of generosity toward others in spite of their own struggles and hardship echoes the message of the Filipino folktale?

14. In Chapter Twenty, Perla and her mother (Aling Lydia) visit Nora's grave house. Nora thinks of Perla: "Maybe I thought her bossiness meant she was mean, when all along, she was just shy, like me." How does this realization change Nora's view of Perla?

15. In Chapter Twenty-five, Tiger is chasing Nora and startles her. She falls back, is knocked out, and awakens inside a tomb. In this scary moment, Nora finds something familiar: "My hand brushed something round, papery. I grasped it between my fingers, feeling the points of dry flower petals prick my skin. *Everlasting.* Even in this dark hole, it was still intact, still whole." How does finding the dried everlasting daisy renew Nora's confidence and courage? In this dire situation, and throughout the story, has Nora herself needed to be "everlasting"—trying to stay "whole" in the "dark hole" it sometimes felt like her life had become? Why do you think the author chose to use the word "everlasting" in the title?

16. In the last chapter, leaving for the hospital to get Mama, Nora observes: "As we pulled away, I realized that my grave house looked brighter. . . . The shadows of sadness were gone and all that remained were the odds and ends of our daily lives. Mama was coming home." Have Nora, and the story, come full circle, with Nora finally seeing her cemetery home, and maybe some of the dark trials of her life, in a new light? Nora still has struggles ahead, but do you think she's learning that broken families, homes, and maybe even hearts can be mended in time?

POST-READING ACTIVITIES
*Take the story from literature to life with these fun
and inspiring activities.*

1. MEMORIES: A PRESENT FROM THE PAST. In *Everlasting Nora,* the author often begins a scene in Nora's present-day life, then something triggers a memory from Nora's past; the narrative moves back in time to that moment, then back to the present. Invite your child to write or tell you about an experience, from their own life, following that format. For example, "I was sitting at school and we were learning about the ocean, and I remembered when our family went on a trip to the beach . . ." Encourage them to "circle back" to the (recalled) present moment to end the story. You and your child might also discuss why memories are so powerful for Nora. Although darker memories can sometimes overshadow her ability to find the goodness in the present, revisiting the happy memories helps Nora feel close to people and places she loved. You can encourage your child to celebrate the present and the past by going on a "Make a Memory" date with family members or friends. Plan a fun outing, trip, or activity, and find or make souvenirs to remind you of your favorite part of the adventure. Then set a date in the future to gather with the same group, share your mementos, and revisit the memory you all "made" together.

2. FOOD FOR THOUGHT. In *Everlasting Nora,* Nora and her mother struggle to afford food, so Nora is often hungry and has a heightened awareness of food, and how various dishes look, smell, and taste, as well as their preparation. The sight or smell of certain foods can also trigger powerful memories for Nora. Invite your child to make a cookbook with you. Ask your child about favorite foods, "comfort foods," and special foods they associate with particular memories, celebrations, or family traditions. Talk about the foods that evoke special meaning or memories for you too. You might also discuss foods that are unique to your family's cultural background. Use your own recipes, consult library cookbooks or cooking magazines, or go online to find ingredients and directions for preparing the snacks, sweets, and dishes you talk about. You might even reach out to friends and relatives and invite them to contribute recipes, with a short explanation of why a dish is special to them. Compile the recipes (annotated with the notes) into a three-ring binder. If desired, your child can decorate the cookbook pages. When guests visit, you can prepare recipes from your "Family & Friends *Flavor*ites" cookbook.

3. **HEARTS AND CRAFTS.** Seeing wind chimes at a street market the day they move from Lola Fely's house to the cemetery reminds Nora of Papa helping her make her own capiz-shell wind chime for a school project. Mama and Nora hang the wind chime in the grave house as a small but powerful reminder of happier times with their beloved father and husband. Invite your child to do an arts-and-crafts project with you, to celebrate a special person or place, as well as being an opportunity for you to spend time working on a creative project together. You might make a Popsicle-stick picture frame to display a picture of the person or event. Place Popsicle (or "craft") sticks in the desired shape and size, then glue together. After the glue is dry, decorate the frame with glued-on beads or shells, stickers, or colorful paint. Another special project you might try with your child is putting together a scrapbook. Discuss special events, trips, or adventures you've shared with family or friends and ask your child to pick one. Together, review, select, caption, and decorate around pictures of your chosen subject. Making and enjoying the scrapbook will give you an opportunity to revisit that special time together.

READING *EVERLASTING NORA* IN YOUR CLASSROOM

These Common Core–aligned writing activities may be used in conjunction with the pre- and post-reading discussion questions above.

1. **POINT OF VIEW:** *Everlasting Nora* is narrated by tenacious but shy Nora. Her age, living situation, and money struggles, as well as being an only child and losing her father and home, shape her view of the events and other characters in the story. Have your students consider how key events or sites in the story might look from another character's perspective. Have students write a 2–3 paragraph, first-person description of life as a squatter in the Manila North Cemetery, from the viewpoint of Mama, Jojo's grandmother (Lola Mercy), or Nora's neighbor, Little Ernie.

2. **COMMUNITIES AND RELATIONSHIPS:** For some, the Manila North Cemetery is just a temporary home; for others, it has been their home for generations. Nora learns that many of the squatters work together as a network of neighbors, a community. Have students imagine they are government officials in the city of Manila whose boss has asked them to write up a report about what is working well, and what some of the biggest problems are, in the community that has developed in the cemetery. Use details from the novel to identify and describe positives (one section) and negatives (one section) in either a two-paragraph, or two-page, report. Ask students to think about the pros and cons Nora and Mama encounter as they adapt to their new life in the cemetery, to inform their report.

3. **TEXT TYPE—OPINION PIECE:** Jojo gets mad at Nora for taking the risk of sneaking into dangerous thug Tiger's grave house to recover Papa's stolen watch. Jojo asks Nora to promise she'll wait for him at her grave house the next morning so they can return to Tiger's for the watch together, but then Jojo sneaks into Tiger's grave house that night to try to get the watch back by himself instead. Have students write a one-page essay

explaining why they agree or disagree with Jojo's decision to sneak into Tiger's grave house on his own to recover the watch. (Remind them to be sure to consider competing factors, like how much Lola Mercy depends on Jojo and how serious the stakes are for Nora and her mother.)

4. TEXT TYPE—NARRATIVE: Have students describe, in the point of view of Jojo, the day Nora arrives at the cemetery. How do they "meet" Nora? What is Nora's attitude toward them? What is her attitude about moving into the cemetery? What is her mother's (Mama's) attitude toward them? Do they think it will be easy or hard to win Nora's friendship? Why?

5. RESEARCH AND PRESENT—HOW DIFFERENT CULTURES HONOR THE DEAD: In *Everlasting Nora*, Nora talks about how her father's passing was marked in her family, and how she and Mama continue to honor Papa's memory and think about his spirit's role in their life. Have students work in small groups to do library or online research into different cultures' traditions around celebrating loved ones who have died, or customs around death that reflect a particular culture's beliefs about relationships between the living and the afterlife. Students might pick from subjects such as: Filipino fortieth-day death anniversary; All Saints' Day (as celebrated in the Philippines); Mexican Day of the Dead; Egyptian customs around mummies, death, and the afterlife; Native American death rites and rituals. After they complete their research, the student groups can organize and present their findings in oral presentations to the class.

6. RESEARCH AND PRESENT—A CLOSER LOOK AT THE PHILIPPINES: Author Marie Miranda Cruz delicately threads local language, customs, and cuisine throughout the novel, making the Filipino culture itself like a colorful banig (woven mat) on which the story of *Everlasting Nora* rests. Have students choose an aspect of Filipino history, geography, or culture, and research it online or at the library. Possible subjects might include: Manila North Cemetery; everlasting daisies; Luneta/Rizal Park and the "flower clock"; Philippine national hero Jose Rizal; typhoons or other extreme weather that affects the Philippine Islands; mahjong; Filipino folktales. Use the research to create a PowerPoint or other multimedia presentation to share findings with classmates.

ENGLISH LANGUAGE ARTS COMMON CORE
WRITING STANDARDS
W.3.1, 3.2, 3.3, 3.7; W.4.1, 4.2, 4.3, 4.7; W.5.1, 5.2, 5.3, 5.7;
W.6.2, 6.3, 6.7; W.7.2, 7.3, 7.7